W9-CLW-918

BLUE
HUNGER

BLUE HUNGER

A Novel

VIOLA DI GRADO

BLOOMSBURY PUBLISHING

NEW YORK · LONDON · OXFORD · NEW DELHI · SYDNEY

BLOOMSBURY PUBLISHING
Bloomsbury Publishing Inc.
1385 Broadway, New York, NY 10018, USA

BLOOMSBURY, BLOOMSBURY PUBLISHING, and the Diana logo
are trademarks of Bloomsbury Publishing Plc

First published in the United States 2023

Original Italian edition published by La nave di Teseo
This edition published 2023

ISBN: TPB: 978-1-63557-949-9; eBook: 978-1-63557-950-5

LIBRARY OF CONGRESS CATALOGING-IN-PUBLICATION DATA IS AVAILABLE

2 4 6 8 10 9 7 5 3 1

Typeset by Westchester Publishing Services
Printed and bound in the U.S.A.

To find out more about our authors and books visit
www.bloomsbury.com
and sign up for our newsletters.

Bloomsbury books may be purchased for business or promotional use. For
information on bulk purchases please contact Macmillan Corporate and
Premium Sales Department at specialmarkets@macmillan.com.

For Martina and Ada

To love is to shed our names.

—OCTAVIO PAZ, *SUNSTONE*

I

Mouth

When Xu bites me, when she has me in her teeth, naked and bad on top of me, everything is good. It's not a human thing but it happened anyway, like a typhoon or an earthquake. It started one November afternoon up against the window of her apartment in Wujiaochang, with the bluish glare of the shopping malls in our faces, and it continued in less private spaces. Former textile factories and slaughterhouses from the thirties, places full of logic and abandon, algid iron architecture, autumn light adrift over derelict sheet metal. I'd been in Shanghai just over a month but already I knew it intimately. Nanjing Road running through the middle like a spine, the dusty suburbs along the Huangpu River, the enormous parks with fluttering flags and peonies as fat and red as newborn babies' heads. The glittering skyscrapers of the Bund and the dry wind blowing west and traversing everything, making it all tremble, the glass and steel and opulent hedges, the deserted industrial parks, the rows of plane trees in the western districts. I'd been there a month and already it felt like home, the way all things that simultaneously suffocate and protect do.

I've never asked Xu if she's done it with anyone else. I've never asked her if I'm the first. But at night when I go with her and her skinny peroxide-blonde friends to the Poxx I find myself apprehensively scanning their wrists, their skin, their slender ankles, in fear of finding marks just like mine. Sometimes a rosy scratch glitters on a finger or the flared edge of a smile. But that's not enough proof; it's nothing. It's hard to see skin well under strobe lights.

I always wind up drinking a little too much imported sake and going home alone, my head spinning. The elegant streets of the French Concession at night amplify my insecurities. Boutiques, bistros, brasseries, backlit displays of plump croissants filled with cream or phosphorescent green matcha. It used to be one big swamp. In the forties the French turned it into a muggy dollhouse full of whores. French law and French lust reigned. Slim bargain bodies dewy with luxe eau de toilette. The bordeaux in crystal glasses a far cry from the chipped cups in working-class neighborhoods, the aseptic perfumeries far from the piss-drenched alleyways and stone drainage canals where children defecated hand in hand. Now it's a chic skeleton of a bygone era. Western businessmen dine on avocado salad and prosecco at café tables alfresco, under rows of illuminated plane trees, feeling special because they live in China, feeling safe because they'll never cross the French border and will never truly be in China.

If I'm not careful I'll go down the wrong road, because many streets in Shanghai have the same name and are differentiated only by North or South, East or West. I need to go East. The ideogram for East looks like a little box with crooked roots growing up through it. But even if I get lost, I still end up at the shops in the Jing'an District, the district where I live. They sell dried beef and steamed buns. Premade pale yellow soup. Disposable razors, single-use skin creams. Face masks whose lids show a purple face, its eyes squeezed shut and mouth open round as if poised to take in male genitals. On the shop ceilings leathery pig heads sparkle.

Her name is Xu but I pronounce it wrong. The tongue should remain still at the back of the mouth where the throat begins, then make a distant, poetic whistle like that of certain nocturnal birds. Whereas I said it like the X in x-ray or xylophone out of a children's ABC book.

A prosaic X, off pitch. This was the cacophonous start of our love. Later I improved and would say "sh" like I was telling someone to be quiet. That was wrong too. I couldn't seem to grasp the true sound of the girl who occupied my mind all day. So I started to stop saying her name. My mouth would open, quiver a bit, then desist: seen from the outside, not saying the name of the person you love looks like gasping for breath at the bottom of the sea.

The cashier is slurping noodles and doesn't hear my greeting. "Ni hao," I repeat. *Ni hao*: it means "You're good." That's how people say hello, with a generic lie about the person in front of them. On the chair there's a white cat on a leash. Motionless, mythological. If I get lost, I always end up at the same convenience store, like a ball landing at the bottom of a pinball machine. I ask the cashier how to get to the Temple of Peace, because my hotel is right across from it. Up on the thirty-first floor, too high for street noise to reach.

The cashier is always the same. Even if I go into a different store. Hard, smooth face, thin eyes. He opens a map on his phone, zooms in and out, showing me things I can barely make sense of. Complicated blue marks on a white background. A route to follow. I find him attractive but maybe that's because I've felt lonely for so long.

If he asks me my name or what I'm doing in China, if he asks me about anything more personal than geography, I show him the ideogram for home on my phone, to say *I'm going home, I just want to go home.* Sometimes the word *home* is nothing more than a need. He smiles. I say thank you and buy a bag of White Rabbit candies. They're wrapped in unremovable, edible paper; your tongue breaks through it to get to the milk. The milk is flavorless. The rabbit on the wrapper reminds me of a stuffed animal I wanted for Christmas when I was five that no one got for me. They got it for my brother. My brother shouted louder, wanted harder, his cries filled entire shopping malls. I arrive at the hotel. This is the place I call "home." The ideogram for home shows a pig lying under a roof: Chinese peasants used to snuggle pigs like infants, with an affection full of angst.

Xu loves few things in this world. She loves silence, lipstick, the stripes of light cast on the wall through half-closed shutters. She loves pork belly in hong shao sauce and she loves to hurt me. Hong shao pork is very easy to make: you slow cook pork belly in wine, oil, soy sauce, and loads of sugar. When it's done, the meat glistens ruby red.

I don't remember what I was like before I met her anymore. I remember the basics, things anyone could know. Like that I'd lived in Rome my whole life and that I watched lots of TV at home on the sofa. I remember that I had two parents whom I loved, still do, and up until six months ago I had a brother too. I remember the brown-edged houseplant—a Chinese money plant—on the windowsill in my room, and the deafening smash of the glass recycling being collected on Corso Vittorio Emanuele. I remember fighting quietly with my mother, quickly tiring, and mid-argument my feelings becoming mechanical, things to which I barely connected. I remember that the place we fought most viciously was my brother's empty room. I remember I had long, long hair and I slept a lot and before going to sleep I'd tell myself I'd water the browning plant tomorrow, I would for sure, but then I never did.

I like the hotel room. It's gray and spare and has fake hardwood floors. There are no curtains or blinds and you can see Shanghai from up high, which is more beautiful than anything I've ever seen. The air ventilation unit, mounted outside the window, makes a despotic whirring noise that never lets up. It penetrates your dreams, like a siren. It drowns out the music when I dream of my brother playing the piano and laughing.

I know that every room on the thirty-six floors of the hotel has an identical unit, and this comforts me: the idea of having something in common with others besides basic human physiognomy. A small painting over the bed depicts an inscrutable object. An animal, maybe, or a landscape hardened by drought. The lines are so abstract you're forced to imagine, but not abstract enough to be relaxing. Sometimes I hope to meet another person on the elevator, but when someone comes in, I get a lump in my throat.

Xu has hair the color of tar and is glorious. Slender hands, moon-white legs. A dark smile just a touch off-kilter. She could play the harp and walk the most applauded runways. She could be a supportive girlfriend, the kind mentioned with teary eyes during family gatherings. She could be a lot of things. She is none of them. She's the person I love. She's the person who can't love me. When her chapped mouth rests on me I think useless things with great intensity, for instance, that language shouldn't come out of the same orifice as vomit and spit.

If I ask myself what I was like before meeting Xu, I think of my brother Ruben's face, his hay-colored hair and straight nose, his reticent mouth, his bright and steady eyes like the neon sign of a hotel after a long trip. I'm used to thinking about him instead of myself. It's easier, because he was better. The fact that he's dead makes this practice more effective.

It's Saturday. It's night. My head is spinning. I put my phone on airplane mode and eat sweet rice cakes the color of pitch. I eat too many. I eat them to the point of nausea. They're spongy and bland and I feel like I'm eating the muggy night on certain narrow streets behind Hongqiao station. That's where Xu and I go to get our yellow pills. The yellow pill is made from snake bile and it inhibits your need to feel safe. It acts on the amygdala; it makes your brain feel like it's padded in a straw blanket. If you take two, you'll even feel safe in the passenger seat of a car driven by a killer going two hundred miles an hour. Xu is my two-hundred-mile-an-hour killer. She's the one who puts me in danger and makes me forget the simple dream all humans share: to be safe, at peace. To be safe and at peace.

It's November 18. Outside the thick glass, a few high-rises switch off, except for the gym where dark female shapes continue flittering like fish. The offices remain dimly lit, a gloomy yellow light which would last until daybreak, and I watch *The Could've-Gone-All-the-Way Committee* on Netflix until I fall asleep and don't care what Xu writes to me.

2

Tears

I arrived in Shanghai on October 2. It was the tail end of the longest summer in the last fifty years. And the one with the most typhoons and rainstorms. One hundred and forty-eight days of humidity (a record for Shanghai) and four typhoons in a row. While I was in Rome handling the bureaucratic side of my brother's death (will, obituary, social media announcements), in Shanghai there had been Lekima and Lingling, Tapha and Mitag. One after the other, their guttural names like portents. Wild onslaughts of wind and dust. While I was in Rome crying my last tears before a certain part of my heart dried out, the part that will always belong to Ruben and Ruben alone, those Asian typhoons brought a third of that whole summer's rainfall. The papers reported that after all that water the autumn would be unusually dry and sunny. Sapped of all violence and feeling. A finale of light and loss, like every peace. A surrender.

I came out of the Pudong airport into a dark fog. It was night. It wasn't night, it was only six P.M. I battled the wind to get to the taxi stand. I missed my parents. But I was twenty-five, past the age for that sort of fearful homesickness. Either way, the most important part of my family wasn't there anymore. Neither in Italy nor in any other part of the universe. My brother. My twin. He'd wanted to be a chef; he'd wanted to live in China up in a high-rise, close to the sky. I gestured to the first driver in the line.

Out the window the city looked too big. It leached out in every direction. The glowing perimeter of skyscrapers, the intricate roads, the icy brilliance of the white convenience store signs—it didn't conform to the idea of a city in my head: it wasn't order but accumulation, like a dream that scatters trauma over random memories, mixing bodies and symbols and images from TV. An unsettling, mournful dream that dissipates upon waking. We stopped, blocked by traffic, next to a huge fairy-tale castle: the Russian embassy.

The taxi driver let me out, pointing a knotty finger past a beehive-shaped building with blue windows to the end of the road. The hotel was at number 199 on a street that, according to the signs, only went up to 129. I walked three times around the block, immersed in a thick cloud of smog and fry fumes. The neighborhood was a warren of towering constructions and little shops. The automatic doors of convenience stores opened and closed on their cold madhouse light. Hands set steamed buns in bamboo baskets in the middle of the street. It was dinner time. Through restaurant windows I saw people leaning excitedly over tables full of food. I lost sight of the beehive building. My eyes searched for it, for the windows, but the blue had vanished.

Twice I passed the store selling shoes that imitated other shoes, and three times by the local SIM card seller. Number 128, 129, then the road funneled into a narrow plaza with a fire station and a row of closed restaurants. I couldn't figure out where I needed to go and my anxiety was mounting. A pink-clad girl with an overly big head stood under a streetlamp shouting across the street to another girl over the traffic noise, and it was a relief not to understand, I was so tired, tired of everything, tired of my brain forcing me to understand things.

Finally I noticed a small wrought-iron gate, went through it, and found the hotel, a 199 tucked between 128 and 129, festooned with flags that fluttered in the breeze. Reception was on the twenty-first floor, obscured by an artificial plant with thick, shiny leaves. The guy at the desk had green hair and didn't really speak English. Obviously no Italian either. His voice was sharp and petulant. I spoke some and gestured some, he didn't understand, and I wanted to cry. I had a reservation. Of course. What name? The Dianzhou language school? No, me. "What is your name again?" I enunciated each syllable, counting out the words like a rosary, dumbstruck by the difficulty, by the expansive desert beneath language. I left a second of silence between syllables so the green-haired boy could find his way along the words.

I wanted to extricate myself from the situation the way I usually did: I didn't give him my name, which the boy kept asking me for with a sheepish look, afraid of writing it wrong, but my brother's. Ruben, Ruben, Ruben. A magic word. He had always helped me with everything. *Ruben, fix the printer, Ruben, fix my mood, cheer me up because I got dumped and I feel alone, because it's raining and the stain on my shirt won't come out . . . Ruben. Ruben? Ruben. Ruben, my hands are dry, my eyes are dry, look how pale I am, Ruben I'm like this fake plant on the desk, I'm . . .*

My lips quivered. The boy repeated, "Sorry," and searched again on the computer. I looked at the plant and it seemed like the boy's voice was coming from those leaves: languid, passive green. I showed him an email on my phone and he found the reservation number. He handed me an iridescent key card.

3

Eyes

I slept for eleven hours. I woke up at six in the morning, exhausted, to the rustle of a newspaper being slipped under the door. I leapt to my feet. A newspaper for foreigners, in English. Glossy pages with lots of pictures. Construction of a 2,135-meter-long bridge approved in Guizhou Province. Storms forecasted. A woman's eyes burst into her towel after a shower at a four-star hotel in Pingyao.

I turned on the faucet and poured myself some water. It had an acrid chemical smell. I didn't drink it. I looked through my suitcase for the Moka pot I'd brought from Italy and used the water I'd bought on the plane. I sat by the window and waited for the coffee to brew. Outside,

Shanghai gleamed with its complex, vitreous beauty. You could see the gold Temple of Peace and Tranquility and the glittering lions at the top of the pillar in front. A blue-gray horizon, punctuated with high-rises and rendered opaque by smog. At ground level, in the streets, a carpet of people in motion. I said to myself, incredulous: *I'm in China.* As if I needed to convince myself that a cardboard backdrop in a school play was real. As if it wasn't my life. In fact, it wasn't.

I dug my phone out of my bag and turned it on. Ten messages from my parents and five from Michele. My ex. Seeing his name on the display sparked no reaction. On September 26, the instant I finished packing, I dumped him on WhatsApp. It was raining and I was in the bathroom sitting on the toilet lid a few hours before my flight. He responded with a voice message eleven minutes long. I only listened to two. His voice was as downy as a freshly mown lawn. He was nice, but nice things were of no use to me anymore.

The heat outside was oppressive. Across from the hotel, the scent of animal fat and cumin emanated from the outdoor grill of an Egyptian restaurant. The narrow street, Yuyuan Road, led to a huge, abstract intersection, towered over by a red-and-gold art deco building. Ornate and decadent, stuck there like the ghost of a place from the past. A 1930s ballroom that went belly up, then a cinema for Maoist propaganda, finally abandoned to itself, a crumbling castle in the heart of an increasingly technologized city. Until one rainy day in 1990 when part of it collapsed, suddenly, like the brittle bones of a dead animal, killing a bystander. Now it was one of the most popular dance clubs. Renovated, polished to perfection, with the portentously sentimental air of the early twentieth century's chaste ballrooms, their unspoken passions. It's called the Paramount in English which becomes Bai Le Men in Chinese, meaning "gate to a hundred pleasures." Every time a foreign word is transcribed into Chinese, it multiplies like a plastic pellet in a kaleidoscope: its original sense, its original sound reproduced in the new language, is augmented by the new meanings carried by each character. A foreign word transcribed in Chinese is a gate to a hundred senses, a hundred pleasures; saying it without knowing what they are is dizzying. I walked past the building, barely able to look away. The Paramount glowed with a soft light, just visible in the blinding sun.

China was Ruben's dream, not mine. He dreamt of it for years. Dreamt of the temples, the bamboo, the grease-painted faces of the Peking opera. Immense, cerebral, sly China. At thirteen he kept all the crumpled messages from fortune cookies: *Friendship is an important value*; *The future will astonish you*. At sixteen he'd buy chopsticks and seaweed at the Asian groceries behind Piazza Vittorio. He wanted to open an Italian restaurant in Shanghai, something elegant and a little avant-garde. Not the usual folksy fare. A place where the food is creative and puts you in a good mood. China. The country of philosophy and sex dolls. They're an essential good: for every 113.5 Chinese men, there are only 100 women—something has to fill the gap. Fill the loneliness. Thousands and thousands of them are sold every year, it's the biggest market in the world. Parted lips, premium silicone skin, languid eyes. They move their arms and say affectionate phrases. They're the most beautiful, the most realistic, the best equipped to free humans from the caprice of loving real people. *I want you, I love you, hold me tight.*

I turned down an enormous street, lined by plane trees wrapped in clusters of fairy lights. I didn't know where I was. Then I saw the sign: NANJING ROAD/NANJING LU. There were two ways to say it, like with every street: the right way and the hybrid, half-English way. I said it twice so as not to forget where I was. Where to go back to when I got lost. I memorized the unicorn T-shirt store. The flag waving on the pole. My globular reflection in the glass: over the last few months, as my brother diminished, taking up less and less space until he died, blending into the granules of earth, I had increased. Over ten pounds. There was something logical about it, like a law of physics, this exchange of weight. Something terrible.

I walked for hours. I followed the trees toward a horizon of steel and light. It was all pretty; there was nothing that wasn't pretty. The big shiny buildings, the groomed hedges, the exorbitant ten-floor stores and window displays filled with lavish flowers. The plane trees with sturdy, eager branches like plastic Christmas trees. I felt uneasy. I was used to interrupted beauty, Rome with its overflowing dumpsters between amphitheaters and medieval basilicas. Whereas in Shanghai the beauty seemed to unfold without impediment, with stifling continuity. Sharp-cheeked models sat motionless on gold chairs, waiting to audition for an imported perfume commercial. Actresses crossed the street dressed in precious 1920s qipaos, hair pulled back, gaze aseptic. Girls with round faces shiny as citrus fruit posed on marble steps in front of posters advertising something in block print. Fathers in shiny loafers snapped photographs. I went into a convenience store. There were pink and yellow dolls on the shelves and ready meals in plastic containers. I pointed to a steamed bun and bit into it in front of everyone; it was boiling hot.

Outside, on the enormous street, the red sky reflected off the facades of the skyscrapers, the squat Gucci and Armani buildings and the sleek multinationals, radiating a sharp, artificial glow like a TV set. It was five, an early sunset for late summer, at least for me with my Italian memories, all the Roman terraces awash with light I had in my head. I was in the city of money and fast love. Of buildings erected so tall you couldn't see the imploring life down below. Where were the beggars, the homeless? Throughout the history of China, Shanghai has always been the city of luxury. Of outlandish fashion, of technology, of the glamorous life. It still was. You saw it everywhere. The sinister sparkle of abundance. The push to rise up out of misery, with diamond-studded wings imported from the West. Worry free. The childlike, omnipotent hope of never again seeing the putrescent side of life. Shanghai was still the richest, most arrogant, most fabulous city. The most ancient Chinese tradition upheld by affluent European hands. My legs hurt but I wanted to get through as much space as possible. Getting through is better than understanding. It's more comforting. Replacing thought with wide, unknown roads. I wanted to go back home, but home was wherever Ruben was and Ruben wasn't anywhere anymore.

I walked all the way to People's Square. A big, chaotic space, dotted with unlit signs. So many metro exits opened up in the asphalt that the square seemed sunken. There was a long, narrow park with open umbrellas all over the ground. I went inside. It was almost dark.

A piece of paper was attached to all the umbrellas. Behind them sat women in their fifites, the humid heat rising from the pavement and sticking to their puffy, square faces. They talked, jittery. They spoke as if vomiting. They had strong arms and sad eyes. I kept thinking about the girl I'd read about in the paper: sitting on the toilet, naked, her eyeballs in her lap, wrapped in a towel like baby birds.

I tried to read the writing on the umbrellas. It was harder in the dark. What was this place? The papers were torn jaggedly and the handwriting was shaky, as if they were pleas for help. I didn't know many words of Chinese, but in the last two months of his life, Ruben had taught me the basic structure of the language. I stopped to read one of the papers on the umbrellas, with difficulty, consulting the dictionary on my phone. *My name is Ling, I'm 30 years old, I like taking walks and going to the circus. If you're tall and kind, you're the one for me. Call this number.*

I read more of the papers. Two, three, ten. They were marriage ads. Laconic and resigned. The women stationed behind the umbrellas, which spanned the entire park, were the mothers of daughters seeking husbands. On every umbrella an appeal for love, crudely affixed with two strips of tape.

I headed home, following the plane trees. Like a map. They were London planes. Patient trees, disease and dehydration resistant. Ideal for being scattered like orphans in a boundless metropolis. Ideal for being left to themselves. Their greenish bark peels off compulsively, a constant rejection, ridding the tree of smog. At a certain point it got too dark and I was exhausted. I hailed a taxi. I showed the driver the address on my phone. He bolted off, turning onto a dark side street. I had read everything about China. To live up to that dream that wasn't mine, act it out plausibly, like an actress with a complicated script in another language. I had studied everything. History, poetry, the genius of the language: a language with many symbols and little grammar, an abstract and musical language, made to communicate with the gods. Out the window, in a flash, I saw a bum sitting on the ground. He was holding a carton of milk. A police officer, from a distance, whistled to chase him away. He darted off and vanished in the darkness. My cheeks burned with guilt, like a fever.

4

Zits

Classes started the next day. I'd taught language to foreigners in Rome, but this time it was different. Italian students in China are the ones who didn't get a high enough score on the entrance exam to study English, French, German. In China, Italian is the language that falls to the losers. I wondered whether my students would enjoy it anyway. Enjoy the fruits of their failure. At eight A.M. I walked the quarter mile between me and the school, fanning myself with a flyer. The sky was murky, permeated with chemical fumes and smoke from the streetside grills.

The school was orange. The bathrooms were orange, with rickety fixtures and over every sink rectangles of residue from mirrors that used to be there. The classroom was orange. As I sat down at the desk and pulled out my notes, a swarm of mosquitoes descended upon me. Mosquitoes always appreciated my blood. I never turned them away. I saw their hunger as a form of love. I saw every invasion as a form of love. It was a flaw I had. On summer nights when I was little, I would open the windows, turn on all the lights, and methodically outstretch my arms and legs for the insects in the vicinity. *Come, little ones*, I'd say, in a low voice so only they could hear.

It probably started in the womb. The fishbowl I shared with my brother. Even as fetuses we are presented with the choice of how to occupy space. The body decides, forms an arrangement, an oppressive harmony. After birth, however, we had to decide rationally. Every single day. Wherever he was, I wouldn't be. One would get the bigger hug, the sweeter attention. The love allotted to him wouldn't go to me. Instinctively, with morbid resolve, I decided I would be the one to take up less space. Everyone else complied with my choice. Ruben got the best Christmas presents and the most French fries. The adults' hopes for the future. There wasn't a logic to it. It was my sacrifice, offered up gratuitously like the severed stinger a bee leaves in an arm before dying.

The students stared at me, confused. Sitting stiffly on their orange chairs. Pencils and notebooks symmetrical on the desks. Electronic dictionaries on standby. Almost all of them were girls. Some pretty, some hideous. Some simply common. They had ruby-red pimples on their cheeks and steady gazes. There was an excitement, orange like the end of a sunset, stamped on their faces: a desire to learn, or maybe just to grow up and find a job. I had taken over from another woman whom I'd looked up on Facebook before leaving: motherly face, sibilant Chilean name, I didn't know what'd happened to her.

In the classroom I pulled out books and markers and did the only thing I knew how to do: teach. Teaching, to me, was not an act of giving, or sharing. It was a way to declutter my mind. I looked at the students, their neatly arranged notebooks. I wondered what it was like for them to pronounce a language other than Chinese. Chinese is tonal: it must have been strange, saddening even, for them to say words void of intrinsic notes, of obligatory musicality.

We began with introductions, all in Italian. "I'm Di," said a willowy girl in the front row. She was very cute and dressed in gray. She seemed uncomfortable. She kept her eyes down.

"What's wrong?" I asked her.

"Our old professor let us use Italian names," she said haltingly, blushing. "Can I be Elena?"

"Yes, sure. You can be Elena. You can be whoever you want."

She smiled with relief.

Since they had a new teacher, they were free to choose new names. Be someone else. A kind of rebirth ritual.

"I want to be Flavia!" exclaimed a girl behind Elena with a broad, prominent forehead. "I'll be Claudia!" another in a polka-dot blouse shouted out eagerly. There arose a buzz as they thought up new names. They pronounced them flatly and intensely, like esoteric mantras. The classroom was bursting with enthusiasm.

The one boy in the class named himself Filippo. I, too, wanted to be not myself but someone else, someone less specific. A polite, gently authoritative teacher like so many others. The kind who wear heels, don't bite their nails, who never say hello first and always reply with a distant but cordial smile. I told them they could call me Xin, which means "new." I told them it was a translation of my name—lying, too, was part of the novelty. As I left the classroom I remembered with chagrin that *xin* also means "heart": same symbol, same tone, like a glass breaking.

I ate cold food in a park full of people. Dead leaves, candy-colored artificial lakes. Children squirmed in the heat like bugs. A thirties song, treacly and indistinct, drifted from somewhere, as if exhaled by the stone lions planted in the concrete. An old man asked me imploringly, in English: "What time is it?" then answered himself: "It's one. Still one." In the distance a policeman whistled in his direction, and he ran off. A sign read: STAY OUT OF WATER.

After lunch I walked over to Yu Yuan, the sixteenth-century garden. Lots of knobby rocks and in one spot a dragon jutting out into the sky, its black jaws splayed. There was an attached bazaar, an open-air funhouse of red pagodas and moldering cement. Paper lanterns. Rubbery eel served in little wrappers. Frozen yogurt. Tea shops that smelled like fruit and jewelry stores, luxury boutiques risen out of the rubble of construction sites.

It was nice not to be in Rome. Rome was where I lived and where Ruben had lived and where he had died and I had kept on living. Of course Rome also had imposing ruins, the stone amphitheaters corroded by time and heat—that is, Rome had its own death proper to its architecture and history that had nothing to do with me or my brother. But it was impossible to separate my emotions from the place in which I'd felt them.

I sat down among the stones while happy strangers took pictures. Chinese skin tends not to sweat. It's odorless but often oily. Sometimes the little zits on the girls' milky faces looked to me like precious gems in the blazing sun and made me want to go up and talk to them. But they were never alone. There were always boyfriends or family, and they sat on benches for hours laughing and eating and singing together. Such long summers lead the already happy to an indolent happiness, with no weeks or horizon. This serenity wasn't going to last for long. The typhoons in July, I'd read in the foreigners' newspaper, had covertly triggered a significant shift. The contrast between night and day was going to become more dramatic. Like two separate worlds, ill aligned. The areas outside the city would be getting colder and colder. Dreams would freeze.

I crossed the Nine Turn Bridge. Water the color of arsenic, plastic lotus flowers. A humpbacked woman with eyes like pits told me that zigzag bridges ward off evil spirits because demons can only travel in straight lines. All those deviations confounded them. The woman was hawking moldy old bracelets. I tried one on, mostly out of politeness, but it fell apart. The woman started yelling. I turned and left. I burrowed into the teeming crowd, hungry for distraction and levity. The little yellow lights on the pagodas' curved eaves switched on. A hand, warm and dry as a piece of bark, grabbed my wrist. "Money, money, money," a voice yelled. It was the bracelet woman. She had a deep, damp mouth, full of rotted teeth. She shoved me and I tottered backward. She said something else, in English, whispering angrily. I didn't understand; I understood perfectly. "Look at you, you ugly bitch."

5

Faces

I woke up to the rustle of the newspaper. It was past ten. In Rome that never would have happened. In Rome my sleep was heavy and impenetrable. Only in Shanghai did the slightest sibilant noise have such power over me. In Shanghai I was always on edge, and my REM phase was so loose everything filtered through. I grabbed the paper. Weather: sunshine, clear skies. Child born without eyes and abandoned, in Nanzhou. His ocular implants had to be replaced every six months so they wouldn't deform his head as he grew. His adoptive mother, in the photo, hugged him with a blank smile, her right hand on his bald white head, which looked like an ostrich egg.

In the shower the words of the woman from the bazaar came back to me. Hateful words, hissed through her teeth. Was it really possible that she had called me *ugly bitch*? No, she couldn't have. I stepped out and studied my image in the mirror. From the neck down—the face was fine, because every once in a while Ruben came out in the eyes, like a stye, a trace of blood and resemblance. I hated the rest. The rounded belly. The thighs. I touched the wavy white stretch marks with disgust. It was no one's fault I hated my body. It wasn't because of my parents, nor my timid and paranoid adolescence, nor even the cakes that every night since the funeral I'd been eating, watching Netflix until I felt bloated and achy in the middle. Maybe it wasn't even because of Ruben, letting himself get sick and die and leaving me all alone. He'd taught me how to make the batter: I mixed forcefully, tingling fingers covered in flour, trying to remember the right amounts of sugar and butter. I'd chew, and I'd swallow, until I felt something, anything. I threw on some clothes.

Class was never-ending. I took a bathroom break halfway through the first lesson to touch up my makeup. I was wearing a black suit. In my compact mirror I could see myself only in pieces. Part of a tit, a leg, a forearm. Inspection always took place in the bathroom. Any would do. Under the harsh lights, against the polished spotless tiles, I pinched my excess centimeters of skin disconsolately. When Ruben was well, I had a neutral relationship with my body. It neither repelled nor attracted me. It was something I had to pay attention to, but not necessarily to the maniacal extent that women usually do. I washed it and fed it and expected it not to cause me undue pain.

In a small temple, on my way home from school, I saw two stocky, silent women on a parapet in the middle of a lake preparing a wavy paper dragon. It was the seventieth anniversary of the Republic of China. A week-long celebration. The lake was murky and chartreuse and the wind that ruffled the paper and the women's hair penetrated my bones. Back in my room I found that Google wasn't working. My VPN got me nowhere. I couldn't look up *how to lose weight fast* and *how to get over a death*. Or watch my shows on Netflix. Annoyed, I went back out. People were pouring into the streets for the celebration. They laughed and tossed balloons, munched on food in paper boxes. It was an intense, mindless cheer.

I turned onto Nanjing Road. An endless street. It seemed to get longer every time I took it. I passed stores selling shiny plastic prayer beads and Hello Kitty hair clips and took the metro down to Century Park, an imitation Central Park. There were lots of entrances, the skyscrapers across the Huangpu River, neat lawns and shiny benches. It had an atmosphere of cold and gratuitous newness.

An emotionless urban simulacrum, like a geometry problem. I entered through gate 7 and came to a fake beach. Children were making castles out of synthetic sand and periodically one would burst into tears and be gathered up in an embrace. Teshigahara made a film that takes place in the sand. In a hole. A movie full of sex and strangeness. The bodies become products of solitude and sticky heat. I watched it with Ruben. I remember it vaguely.

I rinsed my face in the public bathroom, which had only one mirror; the others had been removed. In the reflection I saw myself first, and I looked at her with diffidence. Then I saw my brother, like an echo, the second shadow of my features, and I smiled. I touched my nose as if it were his. "This bridge wards off evil spirits, because demons only walk in straight lines," I said, even though it made no sense.

The day before Ruben's death, sitting on the rigid hospital armchair at his bedside, I read an article that stuck with me. It said that animals sense death approaching as if it were a predator. An invisible predator. This even applies to large animals unused to physical threats. They sense death and allow it to come. Their muscles slacken in the face of inevitability. There's a tenderness, to me, in this, which derives from not fully understanding. We understand (death, love, that love doesn't erase death and death doesn't erase love), but that understanding brings too great a discontent for tenderness. Pain leaves us ragged and graceless. As I left the park, from somewhere in the distance I heard the delicate notes of an erhu, the Chinese violin that intones bygone passions.

6

Bones

On October 31 it was still hot and that's when I saw Xu for the first time. At the Poxx, a club for Westerners in the heart of the French Concession. It was ten P.M. I'd graded homework till late and was starving, and by the time I went out I found all the food places closed. After walking around for half an hour I noticed a fuchsia neon sign between two yellowed trees. I didn't know the place. I just thought fuchsia signs were for non-Chinese spots, and non-Chinese spots often stayed open late. Going down the escalator from Wuyuan Lu, symbolically you left China. At the bottom, it was pure, blinding Occident. China bleached until it became Europe.

On the raucous square there were Irish pubs and cocktail bars and dark dance clubs with flashing lights. Every locale had a glamorous veneer, like the white people inside them standing around drinking, skinny and self-assured, with glossy lips and easy laughter. I would learn many things there. To get so jealous my legs shook. To drink quantities of sake hard for one stomach to handle. To laugh for a long time. To take care of myself without expecting anything in return, the way you do with plants. To hate Xu's friends. To tolerate Xu's friends. To fall in love, by accident, the way you hit on a religious channel while looking for something to watch on television.

I chose the Poxx because it glowed. It glowed brighter than all the other places combined, especially once you were inside. An alarm-blue light, like an emergency room. There were girls dressed as possessed nuns and characters out of Stephen King. It was Halloween, even in China. Maybe even more so. I sat at a corner table and ordered some prawns. I ate, watching the clown from *It* projected on the back wall. The clown appeared and disappeared in the light. Then I saw her. At a table off to the side, alone. Dressed as a fox. The one from Chinese folklore that turns into a woman to seduce gullible, needy men. I vaguely remembered the stories. My brother had told them to me.

It's not true that I remembered them vaguely. I remembered them well. Better than stories I had discovered on my own. Tales about delicate, submissive women who pretended to want love but actually wanted something darker. They had pointy nails and eyes that flickered in candlelight. There was always a moment of revelation. A moment in which the two images—the wicked fox and the amorous woman—no longer coincided, their edges separating like a deck of cards thrown on the floor. And then the irrevocable happened.

The girl took off her mask. A pale and angular face, hair a black bob. Pretty, I thought. I'd been on anti-depressants for six months and everything seemed interesting. She started looking at me. Staring. As if she could read everything in my head. What I loved, what I hated, the idiocies I said to myself in the mirror sometimes like I'd seen people do on TV. *YOU ARE A FORCE OF NATURE. DON'T GIVE UP. YOU WILL GET WHAT YOU WANT.* The useless things that accrue in the mind over the course of a life. Sayings, platitudes. The things Ruben said to me the last day of his life that I'd tried not to memorize. *You can keep my piano . . . Don't ruin it . . . Tune it once in a while . . . Fix the windows in your room, they let in too much cold . . .*

She came over. She sat down on the edge of the stool next to mine. From up close she had full lips and a lanky frame, like something out of a magazine. I couldn't believe she had really come up to me.

"Are you Russian?"

"No."

"German, then."

"Nope."

"English. You're English, that's it. I'd like to go to England, it always rains, I love the rain. When it rains I watch bad movies and eat junk. But I like it, it's a way to be alone, to think. Do you like this club? And China, do you like China?"

Behind that avalanche of English words nothing seemed to move. Her tone was calm and cool. I answered by nodding yes and no, like a little girl being questioned by the police in the middle of the night.

"How are those prawns? Fresh?"

"I don't know."

"Bo-ring! Why don't you want to talk to me?"

I was frozen. I was frozen but the world demanded some sort of reaction. The world was an incredible girl asking me banal questions. Maybe that's always the way the world shows up.

"Well? Anybody in there? What are you thinking about?"

"My brother Ruben is dead."

It was the first thing that came to mind. For a long time it'd been the first thing that came to mind, always, no matter the context. Saying it over and over had made it lose some of its magnitude.

"Huh? Did he die today? Are you serious? My god!"

"No, no. Months ago."

"Oh. So why bring it up now?"

"No reason. I don't know why I said that."

"Maybe because you feel like you want to tell me everything. That's a good thing."

"No. It's not that. I actually say it all the time. Yesterday I told a girl eating ice cream on the street."

"What did she say?"

"Nothing. I said it in Italian. Of course she didn't understand. I do it a lot, really. The last time in Rome, I told a telemarketer."

She laughed. Her laugh sounded nice. It didn't offend me that she laughed at me. At my awkward way of handling my grief.

"You're funny. You should talk more."

"When I talk more, I stop being funny and become . . . unsociable."

"I can see that. You are unsociable. You're unsociable and have blonde hair. And your eyes . . . They're brown, I think. Or green."

"I don't know. Brown. But when I cry, they turn gray."

"Do you cry a lot?"

"Only when necessary."

"I'm going to try and make you cry so I can see them change."

"I'd rather you not."

"Tell me something else about yourself." She folded her hands under her chin.

"What do you want to know?"

"Do you like me?"

"Uh . . . You're so direct."

"I'm Chinese. We don't waste time. Don't you know how fast we can build a hospital?"

She laughed again. It was a laugh full of attention toward me. I couldn't tell what kind of attention. Maybe genuine interest. Or maybe a cynical fascination. Like a child watching ants carrying food only to reach out suddenly and squash them. No matter. Either way was fine. I decided to laugh too.

She was waiting for an answer. I stopped laughing. I chewed my food, took my time. My heart was pounding uncomfortably, and she knew it. She read my discomfort, my excitement. I never would have thought I could feel a physical attraction so strong it could be detected, like a wolf sensing a person's fear. She took my wrist. Behind her there was an aquarium full of turtles with pointy, leathery heads. A waiter went over and chose one for slaughter.

"Want to get a room with me?"

I coughed in surprise.

I peeled the last prawn.

I picked it up with my chopsticks and put it in my mouth, rubbery and limp. I envied it because it didn't have to decide whether or not to follow a strange and stupendous girl.

"Okay, let's go."

7

Heart

The taxi sped through the deserted, rain-bruised streets with stomach-churning technique. It accelerated and braked jerkily as the night around us thickened, swallowing up the closed shops and blue skyscrapers, their pinnacles like knife tips. I had an unpleasant sensation as if everything—the downpour, the blue, the arched concrete bridges, the abrupt lunges of the clutch—were coming into my head and getting stuck there. Through the windows, trails poured off the traffic lights.

Fox talked nonstop. She talked about all kinds of things, animatedly, as the dark city rushed by behind the glass. Her English was pretty good. When she came up against something she didn't know how to say, she fell silent and her face scrunched up until another concept surfaced. She talked about clothes and lip gloss, respiratory ailments caused by pollution, so common in Shanghai, and how if you have one you should never eat seaweed. She said she'd never seen any stray cats in Shanghai. "Where are the cats?" she asked. I couldn't really listen; I just wanted to follow the flow of those phrases, be struck by that sound coming from her throat, that emerged from her body just for me. I'd never had such a physical interest in language.

The taxi stopped. I looked at my watch: it was three—how could it already be three? For a second I asked myself whether it was Italian time, a question that made no sense. As I stepped out on to the dark street, and she handed her phone to the driver to pay, I touched my face to find a tear.

We were in Pudong. The financial center of Shanghai. A new district, made of cold skyscrapers and shopping malls, merging into one another, identical and bright like hospital wards. A district calculated to demonstrate something, the idea of an aseptic, redemptive, to-be-completed future. We climbed a ramp of stairs; we walked in a circle suspended over the sleeping city, the blue and red rocket-shaped high-rises, the occasional car zooming past, the loudspeakers issuing the same minute of tired classical music over and over. The ramps of stairs were numerous and concentric, so geometric they hurt the imagination. On one ramp, an American supermarket shone in the dark where the moon should be. Fox took my hand and said: "I like you too much. I don't know, maybe it's fate. But it's not normal."

Before, it was all rice fields, here in Pudong. Miles of golden fields, the kind you see in movies with long takes and farm workers with sunburnt faces. Now it was the area with the tallest buildings after Dubai. The transformation had been rapid and ostentatious. Eradicating everything, reaching into the heavens with glass and steel, reaching like a demon pleading for light. Now the buildings contained newspaper offices, multinational corporations, TV stations—economic paradise. An erratic accumulation of restaurants and coffee shops and 3D movie theaters. When almost everything was turned off, at night, like that night with Fox, it seemed like the future was holding its breath, waiting, waiting to show you that everything was going to be all right.

We entered a tunnel which led to a shopping center, all the stores closed, and then let out on to a street, bordered by iron railings. We kept on walking, holding hands, lost in the music, which waned on the high notes and then picked up again, formulaically upbeat. She told me about M50, a renovated industrial area. It used to be a complex of factories and warehouses called Chunming, and now it housed over a hundred art galleries. I listened to her and asked her precise, thoughtful questions. I thought it was just chit-chat. But she was laying out the geography of our entire relationship. A relationship that had to be planned like a pilgrimage. Like the Japanese in the seventeenth century: lovers who were disillusioned by life and the impossibility of their passion planned a journey that would culminate in a double suicide called *shinju*: literally, "in the heart."

We got to the hotel. Fox paid at an automated kiosk. I watched her from behind, her shiny bob and her hand typing across the screen. I felt hazy and happy. Perhaps happiness was this: the blurring of borders. No one was at reception. The lobby had a vending machine with instant noodles and lubricant. We waited an eternity for the elevator. I said something I forgot as soon as I'd said it. The paint on the thirty-first floor was peeling off like a scab.

She went into the room and sat on the edge of the bed.

"How did your brother die?"

"What?"

"You heard me. Answer."

I was standing next to the wardrobe, an unpleasant and imposing wardrobe, and I wanted to get this subject out of the way and at the same time talk about it endlessly: since Ruben had been gone there was this messy jumble in my head of my thoughts and thoughts I believed to be his. It was difficult to separate them, difficult to determine which ones I could identify as my own.

"Well?"

"He was born with it. A heart defect. It was the biggest difference between us."

"What do you mean?"

"We were twins. But our eyes were different too, his were blue. And this . . ."

I ran a finger around my cheeks: Ruben's were serious, strong; mine were round and rosy like a young girl's.

"See, I look like a little girl."

"That's a good thing. That's the only time in life when we're beautiful. When we're young and don't hate anyone."

"I don't know about that. Children can hate, for sure."

Her face went cold.

"That's not real hate. It's just love in reverse. It can be turned the right way in an instant, with a word. It's just that usually parents don't want to say it."

"What is it?"

"What?"

"The right word . . ."

She didn't answer. She slipped off her shoes, black wedges shiny like a polished weapon.

I felt an urge to leave. Leave and forget this girl, curl up in bed and do something painless. Watch a show, grade my students' work. I knew that being with Fox wasn't going to be painless. But I sat down beside her and placed a hand on her thigh. The same hand that she had grabbed suddenly in the street and held all the way to the hotel: a hand that had absorbed a kind of promise. When I touched her, I felt a shock.

She turned to me abruptly with a wide, maniacal smile. "*Ma davvero non ti ricordi di me?*" she asked. My heart pounded in my chest. The lights were too vivid. Her eyelids batted the way flies flit around food.

"I don't understand. You speak Italian? Who are you?"

"I'm one of your students."

"One of my students?"

"That's what I said."

"I don't have a good memory for faces."

"I remember you perfectly."

"Why are you only telling me this now?"

"It was fun messing with you. Don't look at me like that! You're so funny when you're mad . . ."

She laughed. Her voice, in Italian, was grotesquely authoritative, like that of a cartoon witch.

"I don't understand why you lied to me."

"Lied, that's going a bit far! Don't be so dramatic. I wanted to talk to you without you being in a position of superiority, as a teacher."

"But . . ."

"You know what I mean. Like someone who's supposed to teach me something . . ."

"I don't think I have anything to teach anyone. I mean, besides Italian."

"Does that seem like a small thing to you? Teaching people to think in another language?"

"I guess not. I'm sorry I didn't recognize you. You didn't talk in class yesterday. That must be why you didn't leave an impression."

"Says the girl who never talks!"

"Exactly. I don't leave an impression either . . ."

She laughed again, sweetly this time. She took off her earrings and tossed them on the nightstand. My perception of her changed from one second to the next: cute and then mean, then cute, then mean, then radiant and hollow like the high-rises out the window. My hand was still on her thigh. It was a different hand, now. Different from a few hours ago. Too pink on her white skin, like something burning.

"Now take off your clothes."

I jumped to my feet. She dropped her phone on the bed.

"What? No. I'm not ready."

"I don't mean to fuck."

"For what then?"

"I can't explain. It's an honesty thing. No secrets."

"What do you mean?"

"It doesn't matter. Take off your clothes or I'm going and leaving you here."

The sweetness was gone. I didn't have time to miss it; I had to undress fast or risk abandonment.

I undid the top button on my shirt.

My hands trembled.

"No. Skirt first. Then the rest. There, good girl."

I kicked my shoes away. They flipped over on the rug. On one of the soles what looked like a drop of dried blood was just a crushed flower. Off went my skirt and then my cotton panties and my blouse. My bra. Fox smiled as she eyed my fleshy thighs, my little paunch, the serrated line under my navel from the elastic. She smiled as she commanded, because she knew my mind was as soft as my body.

"I used to be thinner. Before . . ."

"I know. You look good. This is how little girls should look."

"I'm not a little girl," I said in a minute, shrill voice, maybe the voice I had in nursery school. She started to undress too. She slipped off her latex leggings and jacket and satin corset top. She had an expanse of opaque white skin like the amniotic sac surrounding the bodies of newborns. The stagnant light from the wall lamp, the too high watts, revealed skin without a single mole or blemish. Nothing but milky perfection. I approached the bed. I thought of the word *love* and felt embarrassed.

"What's the last book you read?" she asked, unhooking her bra. I tried to remember, but all that came to mind was a red cover and words crowding the page like ants.

It was as if my life were suddenly shedding details to make room for new ones.

"I don't know. I'm sorry. I can't remember."

"Don't worry. Just making conversation."

"You haven't told me your name . . ."

"Xu. My name is Xu. What's yours?"

"Ruben."

"Wasn't that your brother's name?"

"Yes. Now it's mine."

Xu. All I wanted was to look at Xu and be looked at by Xu. Be touched by Xu. Be commanded by Xu. Being with Xu made my thoughts absolute. Free of nuance. Like a desert at high noon. We lay next to each other. On the Day-Glo orchid duvet, under the stream of A/C. I couldn't stop looking at her. The light, on the basil-green walls, was acidic and insistent. Actually, we weren't right next to each other. There was room for a third body between us. For an instant I imagined it was Ruben's body there.

She talked all night. Without touching me. She didn't want to touch me. I didn't want to touch her. Anything more physical than words would have killed us.

"I've had all kinds of jobs. Shit jobs. I just wanted to get away from home."

"I know what you mean."

"I started at fourteen. Working, I mean. I cleaned stairwells. I'd eat fried frogs at the place next to school and then go to work. I never slacked off, because I knew there were video cameras. There are billions of video cameras in Shanghai, it makes you start acting like a reality star. If you know you're always being watched, you stop being yourself. You become the way others want you to be, you know? While I cleaned the stairs I'd make faces, blow kisses, wiggle my ass the way they like."

"They who?"

She looked at me, perplexed. Later I would learn that to Xu "they" was a generic entity not to be scrutinized. To do so would be too distressing.

"But I had short hair and it didn't look good. I dressed like a boy. So I grew out my hair. I bought tight tops and fishnets. I did some modeling for makeup and lingerie companies. They liked my lips. My cheekbones. I was perfect. I was their little doll. Have you ever seen Molly? The doll they sell on every street in Shanghai? Like her. I was like her. But it didn't last long. They couldn't keep their hands to themselves. Little old men with glittering eyes and fast erections."

"And then what?"

"The night of my nineteenth birthday, on a busy photo shoot, I met Azzurra. No one had remembered my birthday. No one. I'm saying this to explain how I felt. You do things for other people, you suppress parts of your personality, and then no one remembers when you came into the world. Might as well have stayed up in the heavens. Or wherever we are before we're born. Know what I mean?"

"Who's Azzurra?"

She smiled.

"She was a nice, very tall, forty-year-old clothing designer. I followed her to Milan but we fought constantly. I always felt hounded by her judgmental gaze. It's a terrible feeling. It makes you stop being yourself. Like locking yourself up in a room. At least in Italy there are no video cameras. Not so many, at least. Shanghai has five billion, did I tell you that? Yet when a child disappears they're never found . . ."

"What happened with Azzurra?"

"We broke up after two months. I found myself in a strange city with no connections . . ."

"But you learned Italian perfectly. I mean, you sound like a native speaker. You don't need to be taking my class."

"I know. I just signed up so I could practice. I didn't know any Italians I could talk to here. Before you, anyway."

"But what happened afterward, in Milan?"

"I found a job at a nursing home. I bathed the old people and reminded them of their grandchildren's names. I reminded them which family members they loved and which ones they hated. I had all this power over them and I liked that. It gave me a reason to wake up in the morning. You know? If I wanted, I could have turned them against their own children, or anything."

"I hope you didn't."

"You're so moralistic. I know whether I did or not. I don't have to pass some test of yours."

"Okay. Sorry."

"Every morning, the old women cried in the bath like little girls and the old men unbuttoned their pants and said obscene things to me. After two years in Italy I came back to Shanghai."

"In those two years you learned the language better than some Italians I know."

She smiled. Her every smile drew me closer to an unbearable, electrifying place in my mind.

"I'd already studied it before I met Azzurra, actually. I started with a cooking show I watched when I was younger, when I was sad. I don't remember what it was called. There was a cute chef who made these amazing cakes, in every color. In the background you could see a garden, filled with sunshine . . ."

I looked outside: darkness and the countless nause-ating lights in the street. The buildings that now appeared faded and metaphysical, the faintly glowing windows of empty offices, in a few hours would come to industrious, televisual life, made of money and data. Xu followed my gaze: who knows how it looked to her. She had grown up in that city, in that unrelenting darkness. Over all of it loomed the Oriental Pearl Tower: a red orb in steel lattice, topped by a tall obelisk. I had been inside there, one night. One of my first. I was lost. The tower looked like a toy and I found it reassuring. I went inside and took the high-speed elevator, my ears popping from the pressure. On top I walked across the glass floor and observed the distorted streetlamps, headlights. It was all so small, so irrelevant. The buildings steeped in darkness, the shopping malls in violent colors.

It was three, then four. After that quick rundown of her adult life she proceeded to the trivial. From her favorite brand of beef jerky to her tricks for winning mahjong. I had the feeling that she used words like wrapping paper: to cover other, more painful things. I couldn't stop looking at her. Her unbelievable body. Her soft eyes, her perfect shoulders, the comma of her navel. Something didn't add up. She wasn't really naked. Nakedness is a wall. A mystery. It's growing up and feeling shocked to see breasts emerging from your chest like soft bulbs from soil. But Xu felt no embarrassment, she had no imperfections. Nothing to be ashamed of, nothing that could be used to punish her.

At dawn, after that avalanche of words, she closed the curtains and brought back the darkness, the only thing that belonged to both of us. The curtains were somber and thick. They had an irritating geometric pattern, something like the plastic fencing used on balconies to keep cats from jumping off. I heaved a sigh: perhaps it was time. I'd never had sex with a woman and I wasn't sure it would serve my happiness, but I really hoped it would. She was on her side, and I inched closer. I was trembling a little. The contours of her body cut into the dark like ominous mountains. In China, mountains are supernatural places. You climb them until you start to feel other things. See other things. The hermits of Mount Tai would bury themselves alive in damp narrow caves until reality burst open like a rotting fruit releasing its pulp. I kissed her. Her lips were ice-cold. The vent wheezed amid the slow sound of saliva and suction of tongues.

She broke away brusquely and resumed talking. As if nothing had happened. She just wanted to talk, talk until she'd exhausted something, what, I don't know. She talked about tea leaves, how you have to pick them when they're as delicate as a newborn's hair. She talked about her family. She presented them like a family off a postcard, without nuance or interiority. People united by blood and a rudimentary love. Sharing meals, watching television together on the couch. Birthdays, holidays. Something about it was off, trying too hard to stick to the surface. Braces, anniversaries, a gray bunny an aunt and uncle gave her. Her voice rose and fell like the sea on the shore. She talked about her father. About his thick hair and his full and red lips like a rosebud. His collection of Mao statuettes. In brightly painted ceramic, lined up on the mantel. She had to clean them every Thursday when she was little, and she did it with her heart in her mouth, afraid of dropping them. She talked about all kinds of trips, exhaustingly long trips. To the suburbs, to the lush countryside nearby. To Lianhu Village to pick lotus flowers, which she would dry inside her Italian grammar books. To Beijing in winter, in the snow, on a tour, which, before Tiananmen Square, took them to a hotel room where they had to silently observe a sales demonstration for a knife set. A man with green eyes and Chinese features sharpened the knives, describing them melancholically like lost lovers, and then gave everybody one to take home. She kept hers for her entire adolescence, hidden in the linens. Every time she was sad or mad she would open the drawer and stroke it. Slowly, without cutting herself. Until she dozed off. Sometimes she woke up to find it next to her, under the covers. Missing in all her stories was her mother. She'd say "the three of us went" but never mention her. She was a tacit presence, like passing time, like the ground we tread. Like air. Like smog. Behind the drawn curtains was the sun, the day, but we were in the dark, trapped in a primordial night, from which there was no way out except a colossal Big Bang.

I could have been more empathic, pushed her to say more. Asked, *What about your mother?* Made her dig deeper. But I could hardly bear her communicative need, that deluge of information with only the occasional flicker of real feeling, taking all the attention from me. I wanted to be seen. Heard. For once in my life. I was repulsed by the feeling, but I couldn't help it. My need for love battered my heart like a homely dog pawing at a door that never opens.

I went back to my spot on the other side of the bed. The rock-hard mattress pressed into my back. Everything was too cold and too clean. It was a bed in a hotel room, a place where nobody actually lives. "Are you okay?" she said. I shook my head. I reached for her, but she got up and opened the curtains. Light flooded the room. It was day again. This time for real. It was eight in the morning. I had to go to work. The kiss had gotten lost in our conversation like a button between the folds of a couch.

Outside the windows you could see cars and pulsating traffic lights, without the audio. At that height, none of the street noise could be heard. Only the air vent. A low buzz replacing the sounds of life. Instead of car horns and engines and torrents of voices, a deep monotone hum: existence from above. The night up there had been soundless. Nothing but me and Xu. My breath, her voice. Now it was louder because it was morning and everything on the thirty-first floor was open. The nail salons, reception, accounting. I thought of iridescent finger-nails in neat rows. Orderly lives. Xu put her clothes on and everything was back up and running.

I was first to leave. In the nail salon, a woman with pockmarks slept slumped over in a child-size chair in front of magazine ads taped to the wall. Turning right, I came to the reception of another hotel, an elegant man in the glow of a blue sign, and then to the sleeping pock-marked woman again, so I went the other way and this time it was the right direction. I sat on a couch and waited for the elevator. On a screen, indistinguishable girls danced in bridal gowns. Translucent skin, glacial eyes, cobalt-blue contacts. They sang "Ode to Joy" in Chinese, their lips parted slightly, looking into the lens with blank conviction, surrounded by walls of lace and cream.

I retraced my path from the night before, but it seemed different. Tourists with SLR cameras around their necks strolled sluggishly in the sticky heat, their faces furrowed, worn. Even the high-rises in Pudong, during the day, were different. Less poetic. There was one shaped like a bottle opener that in the blazing sun appeared excessive and grotesque, like a joke told too late at a party. Even the Oriental Pearl Tower, with its cartoonish silhouette, by day was too outlandish, too expressive. I took line 2 of the metro from Lujiazui. It was packed. Bodies squeezed together, silent. Suffocating.

Outside my hotel, a woman in an undershirt pulled a nearly dead man on a cart. Eyes closed, face dirty, the man lay on his side and seemed to gasp for air. At the sound of a jingle, the woman waved a printout of a QR code to donate money by cell phone. Occasionally she raised a hand and motioned along with the music. I spent the day trying to grade homework, but couldn't concentrate. That night, I couldn't sleep.

8

Lung Pieces

I woke up out of it, at noon. Light was everywhere. No newspaper, because it was Sunday. Without the paper I had no desire to get out of bed. Not because I wanted to read the news, but because I liked the fact that the paper came to me in my room, like someone who comes to check on me and never forgets. I picked up the framed photo I kept on the nightstand. Ruben and me in the forest in Tuscany. But the glass had cracked in transit. Even though I'd packed it wrapped in a scarf and a wool hat. Even though it was my dearest possession. The crack climbed from the bottom up between us, thin as a teardrop, stopping at his face. That photo was the first thing I saw when I woke up and the last that I looked at before going to sleep. Sometimes it was nice to look at and other times it was draining. I turned on my phone: nothing from Xu. *"Ruben, make Xu send me a message,"* I said, staring at him until the treetops in the picture turned paranoid green and his face blurred.

I remembered that in Chinese *forest* and *cemetery* are sometimes said the same way. Remembering Chinese words had more to do with my brother than with my present life in China. I spent the ensuing hours skipping through Asian TV shows and eating dinosaur-shaped candy. After a few lines from a character my mind would wander and start rehashing the previous night. From the conversation at the Poxx up to the kiss. The kiss was a mistake. It erased our distance. Our distance was a safe place. At five the phone buzzed. A message on WeChat, the only Chinese app, which is used for everything: chatting, buying things, showing ID. It was Xu. My heart was in my throat. *Let's go to dinner. I'll be waiting for you in an hour at exit 5 of People's Square station.*

I took the metro to People's Square. It was gigantic, tentacular. I went through the whole place, battling the crowd, in a flickering brown light that reminded me of a box of chocolates, but I couldn't find Exit 5. The directions were misleading. EXITS 1–14, the sign said, but after a row of handbag and clothing stores it skipped from

4 to 8. I had a headache and was starting to get anxious. After three fruitless trips that led back to my point of departure, the numbers became meaningless. I went out onto the square, exasperated, and looked around. Finally I saw her, past a fountain, sitting on marble steps lined with ornamental silicone rabbits. She stood up and gave a little wave.

She was dressed in eco-leather and voile, all black, her skinny legs like sticks wrapped in fishnet stockings. On one wrist, a chipped jade bracelet that glinted in the sun. She smiled and said "Ni hao." It's wonderful, the Chinese greeting. Saying "You're good" affirms not only another person's presence, but also their adequacy. You're good; you're fine: the character represents a child and mother. But the mother's back is bent unnaturally. She is at the service of the child. Her love takes the form of penitence.

We walked under the taut, almost transparent sky. She told me about a new club in the city. She was different from yesterday, less prickly and kinder, more attentive, as if the Xu from yesterday was the real Xu, and today was Xu as depicted by someone who loved her. We walked close, smiling. Everything was beautiful. I felt stunned by the serenity. As if something inside me that had been fidgeting for so long had finally settled.

She led me to the underground level of a shopping center. There were all kinds of places to eat. She chose a traditional restaurant and ordered for us both from a big screen at the entrance, pressing on glowing pictures of intricate, garish dishes. We ate fried bamboo, flower gelatin, egg gelatin, Tibetan mushrooms, mixed tubers, lettuce with mayonnaise, broccoli in cream sauce. The plates were ceramic, dragon-shaped. I didn't like any of it. But I kept on eating and watching her eat. Obediently. Bite after bite. Consuming food she chose was a form of fidelity I hadn't anticipated but that came naturally to me.

The food kept coming. Steamed dumplings, to douse in vinegar. Warm fruit salad. Pork in a glassy glaze. I knew that for the Chinese ordering more than necessary was a principal way of showing kindness. Seducing a person with the promise of endless nourishment. It was an awkward, bulimic form of love. It was something I could understand. I took a breath and kept on chewing.

I wondered what Ruben would have thought. Which dishes he would have admired, how he would have savored them slowly, thinking about how to reproduce them. The afternoons when he baked were the times we were the closest. Remembering those hours, the smell of caramelized sugar, the warm crust melting in my mouth, his look while he awaited my verdict, gave me a pang in the chest. I was full.

The last plate was a dish of dark meat sprinkled with little green triangles.

"Eat."

"I can't. Really."

"Bullshit. You have to try it. It's fuqi feipian."

"Uh . . . Husband and wife lung pieces?"

She laughed.

"Good, your Chinese is improving. Yeah, that's what it's called. It's kind of a joke. It refers to the couple who invented it, cooking together every day. They bonded over slicing meat."

"What is it?"

"Ox heart, tongue, tripe, enough spice to make your mouth go numb."

"I don't know. It freaks me out. I've never eaten internal organs."

"You're always so dramatic, my god. Focus on the taste. You'll recognize the heart immediately, it tastes stronger, sadder."

She pointed to a dark skewer of crimped meat with furrows and hollows. I lifted the stick, closed my eyes, and brought the heart to my mouth.

The restaurant emptied slowly. Someone cleaned a wall in back. We talked about the director Zhang Yimou. About the young Gong Li, round-faced with braids, traveling the unpaved roads of a China that no longer existed. I hung on her every word with painfully intense interest.

"You're pretty, teacher."

"No, I have a common face."

"Exactly. It's nice, being common. They never let me."

"Who?"

"Everyone."

"Everyone who?"

She motioned pointedly for the waitress to bring the check. Then she looked at me with an expression that contained many things. Maybe even contempt. But perhaps I was still unable to read her face.

"You ask a lot of questions. Like you want to crack my head open and look inside."

"No, no, I . . ."

"You have to give me my time."

"I'm sorry, I just wanted to make conversation . . ."

"That's no excuse. You have to act right. Understand?"

I nodded.

I sensed something aberrant about her reasoning, like a speeding car that periodically veered off the road.

"Xu, do you ever feel lonely?"

"Sure, everyone does."

"Some more than others."

"You have something on your face. Next to your mouth. I'll get you a mirror."

She pulled out a plastic Hello Kitty compact. I wiped my face, carefully, shooting glances at her. She had a perfect, sculptural head. I imagined it in a glass case with a descriptive plaque. I imagined touching the glass, mindful of that distance. I'd never thought about anybody's bones before, but Xu's were perfectly proportioned. High cheekbones, small head, slight chin. Looking at those bones, the things she said seemed less unreasonable: her body compensated for her mental cracks.

"Finish your sake. I'm taking you home with me."

I didn't care if Xu's mind was a racecar that might suddenly skid into a ditch. I didn't care if she was out of her mind, out of control. I wanted to be the bumpy asphalt that car skidded on. I wanted to be the ditch, the maddening bumpiness, the rut interrupting the wheel's perfect propulsion. I wanted to become her nagging obsession. Keep her awake at night, keep her eyes agape. Fill her mind like an airbag that expands on impact. But I knew it wouldn't happen. It would never happen. I could never become an obsession to anybody.

It's a talent. A talent I don't have. Ruben could make anyone fall in love with him. He didn't even have to try. It happened. It was a mechanical consequence of his perfection. He exuded beauty and confidence, something trustworthy and carefree. He lopped off hearts like weeds in a garden. I was the one who went unnoticed. A variation of Ruben, his deviation, his faded copy. I was the one who at twelve, thirteen, fourteen, fifteen telephoned his girlfriends, fully trained. In a tone of studied dismay, I repeated the memorized formula: "I'm sorry, my brother doesn't want to see you anymore."

9

Teeth

Once we got off the metro, we crossed a mile of identical streets studded with convenience stores. Pale green signs, automatic doors that opened onto gleaming shelves. We passed Fudan University and entered an austere building. Sixth floor out of thirty-nine. Out the big windows we could see Wujiaochang, the alien egg–shaped hub of shopping centers that never closed. It was four P.M. and the egg was illuminated with transverse blue veins that flashed erratically.

The apartment was small, despite oversize windows, and it seemed familiar. The plastic table, the bright kitchen, the metal light fixtures. Maybe it seemed familiar because it contained simple furniture, without character.

It recalled the decor of a doctor's waiting room, chosen to keep destructive emotions like panic at bay.

I wondered how many other girls had been there, holding Xu's cold hand in the elevator and then coming to that apartment, feeling at home just because it was a house that could have been any other, feeling reassured merely by a combination of materials and colors that absorbed bad omens.

"Have you had lots of girlfriends?" I asked, in Italian. Now that I knew I could, I took refuge in my native tongue.

"*Fidanzate*," she echoed mockingly, as if it were the title of a cartoon. "You're funny. So sentimental!"

I felt a rush of shame. Maybe I should have said it in English. In English, *girlfriend* can also mean "friend." It's a bit safer; ambiguity shields you from disappointment. In Chinese, *nupengyou* is "friend" too. Among the languages Xu and I had in common, only Italian described relationships with such an unequivocally intimate word, sticky like hands intertwined under a bedsheet: *fidanzate*, a word that derives from *fiducia*, "faith," "trust."

I followed her down the narrow gray hall. On the wall hung a poster of the *Edmond de Belamy,* the first painting made by artificial intelligence. A clergyman with a blurred-out face, as if something were missing. And there were two big nails, unused, that had made large cracks in the wall.

In the bedroom, she switched on a lamp. I squinted to get a better look at her things: piles of makeup, a cupcake-shaped pillow, crumpled magazines on the floor. There was a darkness, tense and full of apprehension, like a sick child's room with the shades drawn.

"Could I open the window?"

"Why? Should I turn down the air?"

"It's a little musty in here."

"You can't open the windows. It's too smoggy outside."

As my eyes adjusted to the darkness, I started to notice the food. Open bags of chips scattered across the floor. Cups of juice. A half-eaten apple, browning in the hollow of a ripped armchair. Ramen twisted around the computer keyboard. Shimmering lychee, still fresh, mixed with plastic necklaces in a jewelry box.

"Xu, can I help you clean up?"

"Clean up what?"

She looked at me, perplexed. She took off her shoes.

"The food. Throw it away."

"You don't understand. I need it. I need it around."

Now I could see everything. The brown bananas hanging on a wall hook. The snack cakes and dirty spoons. Stalks of celery piled on top of a book. Lollipops bright as roadside reflectors. Chicken feet in a transparent bowl. Bottles of plum wine and jars of glazed cookies. A pale pink cake caved in from the heat. Even before wondering what the purpose of all this was, this accumulation of food, this leaving it to molder and rot, I wondered how Ruben would have salvaged some of it to create an incredible dish. A surprising, spicy confection, a revelation. A complicated, unrecognizable crepe. But Ruben was gone and all over the world food was going bad, withering and darkening until it lost all shape and appeal. I undressed, nervous, as Xu undressed too.

"What are you looking at?" she asked, her voice hard.

"Nothing. The food."

"Don't think I eat all that. It just keeps me company."

"I wasn't thinking that. I was thinking it's not sanitary . . ."

"Look, I eat it but then I throw up some of it. Being pretty is important to me, it's all I have. So don't worry."

"That's not what I meant, I was worried about hygiene, just that . . ."

"You worry too much. Shut your mouth. Don't judge me."

"I'm not judging you, you're not listening . . ."

"Shht."

Our clothes dropped to the floor like fruit peels. Surrounded by plastic wrappers and straws, raspberries in little heaps on the rug. She crouched over me.

I saw the mirror. A modern design, with ribbons of red candy hung over it. I saw my midsection reflected there and thought that in Xu's mouth it must have the texture of a chewy, artificial confection, with predictable industrial sweetness like the Italian snack cakes from my childhood. It was a new and strange thought, a thought inspired by the putrid embrace of all that leftover food. I imagined Xu vomiting it all up except for me, remaining inside her forever, undigested and safe. I laughed out loud as Xu approached. A hearty, liberating laugh. She took a cookie from the jar on the nightstand and popped it in her mouth. She turned to me, crumbs on her lips, and said, "Lie down." I fell back on the bed and she removed my bra, my only remaining garment. Her head hovering over me, she scrutinized my body.

"Eat me," I said. The idea was mine—it was the first time I'd had a thought like that. I was the first to think of my body as brainless pulp. *Eat me: make me yours, make me disappear.* Something had happened. Something inside me had worked loose, revealing a strange part of the mind. Xu took my breasts and bit my nipple. Was it just a meta-phor, what I said to her? The ultimate metaphor for our relationship? I'm still trying to figure it out. But under-standing is a cold exercise. Understanding is the opposite of hunger. The opposite of desire. Xu bit me again. A rivulet of dark blood, warm like chocolate sauce, trickled down to my navel.

"Go over there," she said, pointing to the window seat. She pushed the curtains aside. The blue of the egg flooded the room. A convulsion of aggressive, alternating light. I saw more food. Brown strips of jerky in cello-phane on the floor. A hard-boiled egg by the wall coated in dust and fuzz. Out the window I saw the street we'd just taken here. The black cement and the corner stores. But it had become a street in another city. I leaned back, the glass against my shoulder blades. I sensed the oscillating blue rays on my cheeks and eyes. She resumed biting. They weren't affectionate or even passionate bites. They were cold, precise, like a surgeon trying to extract an object from the flesh. Her teeth moved from my chest down, lingering at the softer spots.

Then I saw the photos. Photos everywhere, tacked to the walls. Photos of girls. On a bike, by a river. On a pink bed, in a park. All pretty, though unkempt. All smiling. But the longer I looked at them, the further I plunged toward orgasm, the more each grin seemed like an uneasy grimace. Then I saw the bracelet. Three different girls were wearing the jade bracelet that Xu always wore. Sure, it was a common bracelet, the translucent jade band; I'd seen it in practically every jewelry store, but it was chipped in exactly the same spot. Had she slept with them too? Was she showing off her other lovers, the other bodies she had invaded and nibbled, docile bodies like mine, companion bodies? Did she want me to know I wasn't the only one? How did she choose us? The softness of our skin, the sadness in our eyes? She smiled, her eyes crinkling, mimicking emotion. A line of blood fell like a tear from my nipple to my genitals. I was about to ask her who those girls were, floating in the shadows over the scraps of food, seraphic and fragile as sacrificial lambs. I was about to come. The darkness around me vibrated as if something calm and cruel—something that knows everything, and wants to crush everything— were closing in.

10

Stomach

In the days that followed I was elated. The reason why disturbed me a little—that my happiness was the result of Xu's teeth, her saliva—but not too much. The important thing was that I felt good. So good, incredible. After months, years, maybe. I'd forgotten what it was like. The thought of her other lovers dissipated. They were irrelevant. Now Xu, for mysterious reasons, had chosen me. There was only me. I was so excited I couldn't sleep at night, and at school during the day, work was a breeze. The joy was physical, total. A cloud of warmth and openness from my vulva to my head, a wild and melancholy joy to be Xu's repast. Would I have felt the same without her biting me, if our bodies joined in a more pacific, neutral way? There was no way to tell. I asked Ruben, his picture with the crack in the middle, and waited for an answer.

Since I was happy, I was nicer to my students. Since I was nicer to my students, they loved me. Since they loved me, I tried to love myself. Saturday morning, I went walking alone down Nanjing Road, smiling: solitude, once a dangerous thing, had become a space for the imagination. I bought hand-knit sweaters on the seventh floor of the Jing'an mall for when the cold came. I listened to gloomy folk music under the trees in the square. I put on iris-scented perfume in the morning and got massages at Crystal at six. I bought ridiculous undergarments with ice creams and rainbows on them: contentment altered my personality in unexpected ways. At night I waited for my phone screen to light up with Xu's words the way prisoners wait for the morning sun to shine through their bars.

During the day we didn't see each other much. She changed classes, to avoid creating complications, so I saw her only in passing, between lessons. A black crown in the courtyard, from the back, luminous in the blazing sun, surrounded by others in the midst of conversation; I approached with my heart in my throat, but the girl would turn to reveal a different nose, different eyes: someone else. It always took me a few fractions of a second to realize it wasn't her, that she couldn't materialize out of nowhere just because I wanted to see her. It rained for days, a heavy, dirty rain full of dust.

Come sundown we'd go all kinds of places. The music box museum, deserted, all to ourselves. The pearl market, with pearls that looked like teeth hawked underground between knockoff Converse and brightly colored luggage. We'd walk for hours along Duolun Road, the elegant street where writers lived in the twenties, who've now become bronze statues sitting on bronze benches across from each other, absorbed in otherworldly conversation. Two trans girls, gorgeous in traditional pink silk dresses, posed for pictures at dusk, their amber skin radiant outside a brick building. Euphoric, we went back to the Bund, the waterfront view of the Pudong skyline where you can take cheesy photos for a few dozen yuan: her squeezing me as if she really loved me, me looking into the lens, grinning with shyness and trepidation. On the street with restaurants from all over the world we drank beer at the English pub and ate turtle at the Chinese place. Sometimes it all made my head spin: there was too much scenery, too many visual stimuli. A cascade of conflicting urban elements. Shanghai, unlike Western cities, which proceed with restful coherence, unfolds like a dream, an accumulation of images. When you wake up, when you return to yourself, your temples pulse like an alarm.

I went to the restaurant bathroom, but it had squat toilets. Those holes in the ground repulsed me, the idea of opening my legs and watching my own stream of urine. The last time I thought I saw flecks of hot pepper. I decided to hold it. It was Friday again. It was still raining, and I was exhausted. The turtle had an acrid taste, it lingered on the tongue and in the throat. The taste of a creature that lived in the comfort of a shell from which it was yanked in order to be devoured. Ruben never would have eaten it. I never would have. We had a pet turtle for a while, when I was five. Sometimes it slept with its head and legs outside its shell, resting on little piles of grass, as if it trusted fate completely. If you reached out to touch it, it would extend its head to be petted. In an instant, with a flash of animosity, I thought of Xu's lovers from the photographs, of her fucking them. Of that jade bracelet clinking against the headboard, on the wrist of some random naked girl being fucked, like teeth chattering in the cold. I thought of that and I skewered the turtle in its murky sauce. It was the reflection of a thought, the unhealthy shadow of a fear. I chewed. I swallowed. I wish I hadn't. Its innocence burned in my throat.

After dinner we went to a bar where there was dancing. I was a little drunk and couldn't take in much of what I saw. The people danced stiffly, without touching, under the strobe lights. Chinese club music was infantile, repellent yet sweet like finding your baby teeth in an old jewelry box. On the way home, in the taxi, I noticed something moving on the driver's head, wriggling through his sparse, graying hair. A little white grub. I nudged Xu, who was dozing off, and asked her if I was seeing right. She nodded and closed her eyes again. The city outside was immersed in a storm and the astral casino light.

II

Fingers

The body is an anomaly. Matter aggregates more easily in vegetal combinations. Plants constitute 99 percent of earthly matter. Mute matter. It's only a glitch that we have flesh and voice, an inconvenient contradiction in a planet of immobile life. An organicity that shouts, cries, wants, is afraid of death.

We fucked in the bathroom at the 3D cinema.

We fucked in motels.

We fucked at her house under the rays of the alien egg after eating takeout from three different restaurants.

We fucked on full stomachs, in carb comas with the floor plastered in paper wrappers and dirty chopsticks and soy sauce packets.

Getting to know her body and mine at the same time was a destabilizing and exhilarating experience.

Until then I'd paid my flesh the attention one gives a cheap, short-term rental. Now, suddenly, it was different. Xu's hands measured me. They probed me. Like a product off an assembly line that has to be checked before it can be put out into the world. There was something tender about it. Something that moved me.

In her room it was hot, then cold; then time slipped away. She kissed me until I couldn't breathe. I didn't need to anymore. I felt nothing for the world: what emotions I had left I buried in Xu. At six we went to the huo guo place downstairs. It was raining softly. Across a big black table, we plucked thin strips of raw meat and dunked them into the pot of spicy broth. At night, up against the window, I was drunk and happy, my fingers inside her and my eyes closed. I was drawn to the idea of a sterile love, where no level of passion could produce new life. It was a poetic idea. Bodies that join like that, without the subconscious implication of procreation, are poetic bodies.

I liked it when she lifted my shirt and found the soft flesh on my belly. I, who did not feel especially attractive, offered it up to her with a mixture of gratitude and shame. She told me she liked me. I replied that I liked her too. That was it. There was no TV-show sentimentality; there were words only to the extent they held up, past which point they'd crumble, as happened for instance when she asked me about my brother or I went home and she turned off her phone and disappeared for two days while I ate alone, in bed, all night, till morning. Oreos, Kit Kats, cinnamon cookies. Hard crumbs on my legs and under my ass, on my hands, all over the sheets. I checked my phone constantly. Sometimes I'd text her a heart as a last resort, and wait with bated breath. I wondered how many hearts, at that moment, had been cast in chats like bait to sea in a squall. How many other hearts would go unanswered, unattended. The heart, that little symbol with a point and two curves on top, is the most common ideogram on planet Earth. We draw it as children, gratified by how easy it is to trace. We replicate it on greeting cards and defibrillator machines, on the trinkets we put around our necks or tie to babies' wrists. The shape comes from the seeds of silphium, a now-extinct plant that the Ancient Romans used for contraception. Legend has it that the seeds first sprouted on the shores of Cyrenaica two and a half millennia ago after a black rain.

At six P.M. one Thursday, while I was on the metro coming back from the supermarket, she sent me a message, in Chinese. I opened the app, my heart racing, to translate it. It said *me too*. I searched our recent messages for one related to such a response, something left hanging, but there was nothing. Everything was concluded. There were no gaps in our chat. Xu had just mistaken addressees. Someone else, somewhere in Shanghai, was waiting on the conclusion of an exchange with Xu. It was a small thing, but it had a depressive effect. I missed my stop. I sat there for an hour, incapable of moving. I was surrounded by ebullient girls in polyester dresses summarily replicating Qing-era costume. Iridescent jewelry, flower barrettes. I got off and got on another random train. My sense of orientation and rational mind had been replaced with a current of darkness that drowned out my will and all the space around me. It was too hot on the other line. The train was crammed with girls in uniform on their way home from school. They laughed, huddled around pink smart phones. To them it was just another Thursday.

I got off twenty stops later at a place called Songjiang, a big suburb with wide streets. I followed the crowd through ancient red gateways and past big buildings from the seventies and came to a Taoist temple. It had little rooms with cow-faced statues. Animals with wide nostrils and fierce eyes. One had a tongue so long it reached the ground. The place was very quiet and smelled of cinders. They gave me some incense but when I tried to stick it in the sand to pray, it broke apart and the clerk yelled at me. I left, hanging my head. Behind a red-and-yellow barricade in the courtyard bleated a goat lying in its own excrement.

Two days later Xu took me to the fake market, where they sell all kinds of knockoffs. We rode the metro to the Science and Technology Museum stop and spent hours underground between fake Chanel bags and fake Gucci bags, snickering. Then we came out onto the breezy street behind the museum, with neat hedges and high-rises the color of venom. At the end was Century Park. We rushed through before it closed, looking at the faraway boats and toothy outline of the buildings in the distance. I took her hand as we ran, instinctively, and she held fast to mine. When I was with her everything seemed exciting and meaningless. Not like real life but a charming, mediocre film. A blockbuster with perfect lighting and bad dialogue: a movie that sucks you in and then ends badly.

We collapsed onto a bench. A family passed by all strollers, kids, balloons. They shouted, laughed loudly. In the distance, someone was singing Peking opera and someone else was playing the flute. Chinese parks held an exaggerated, polyphonic joy that seemed correlated to centuries of fear and famine.

I went to kiss Xu, but she shrank back.

"Not now."

"Why, because we're in public?"

"No, dork, that doesn't matter. If you want, I'll strip naked to show you how little I care about what people think."

"I know that. I'm just asking."

"Because I decide when we come together and when we stay apart. It's all part of a plan."

I looked down. I said nothing.

Xu placed a hand on my cheek. Her touch was stiff and imperious, like the pat you reward a dog with for staying put.

That night, as I brushed my teeth, I noticed the smell of my skin was different. It was intense, like a well too deep for light to reach. In the last month I'd eaten, besides the usual grayish sprouts and pickled tubers in pungent sauces, too many dried feet contracted by pain. Cleaved stomachs, metallic-tasting livers, tiny unheeded brains. For a whole month I had ingested bodily insides. I took a long shower, waiting for my pulse to slacken. I collapsed onto bed, my face pressed into the pillow. I dreamt it was very windy and someone said to me: *I'm sorry, your brother doesn't want to see you anymore.*

12

Napes

For a while, we went to the Poxx every night. It'd been Xu's favorite hangout since she was a teenager ditching school. Back then it was also open during the day and there was a back room where you could play computer games and drink soy milk in little glass bottles. There were no expiration dates; it was good until the taste made you sputter. That first night, she'd introduced me to her friends. They were always with us, at the club. With her. Like groupie shadows. I hated all of them at first sight. Their salon-styled hair, their jasmine-scented napes. It wasn't jealousy. It was something even more primitive. Innate competition among animals, in the jungle, where everyone's a potential enemy. Some were my students, but the moment we stepped through the door the hierarchy of our relationship collapsed. We were all defenseless in the Western club, under Xu's eyes: we were appendages of her gaze. I didn't look them in the face. I perpetually forgot their names. They were fake anyway. English names, meant for people who would never actually know them. Every Chinese person has at least two names. Their real, private one, for other Chinese people or lovers. And their superficial, Western one, to rattle off for everyone else.

There was the statuesque Kelly, with traffic-light yellow ribbons of hair that hung to her butt. Kelly was also called Biyu: her real name, which I'd overheard in conversation. Biyu also went by Angélie in her French class. Each of these girls was an enemy because they had too many names and too many possibilities, too many chances to become objects of Xu's love. And Xu looked at them with curiosity and affection, she was like everyone's strict yet forgiving mother. The attractive mother, perpetually detached but willing to be distracted from herself for a moment to bestow upon someone the honor of being heard. Technically their peer yet completely distant from the elements of age, demographics, the constraints of being born at a certain historical time. She solved their relationship problems, declaimed Dante, taught them Italian profanities and complicated Chinese recipes. She laughed with her teeth touching, holding a wine glass stained with dark lipstick. They looked on with admiration and attraction. They waited for their turn to share their little quotidian existential problems with her. Crushes, bad grades, parental conflicts. They were waiting to be understood. She understood them perfectly, but didn't want to be understood by anyone herself. She made sure to be incomprehensible. Maybe she thought that if someone understood her, they would know how to hurt her. She had to be the only one to do the understanding, the hurting laugh or listening to the others, under the cloying blue lights of that ruinous place, she would shoot me a distracted glance, but never said goodbye or asked me to stay.

Walking home from the Poxx was like a nauseating journey into myself. Drunk, I could easily mistake a Chinese girl with short blonde hair, from behind, for my brother. Mistake a slender, pale hand holding a cell phone for his. The same way I often mistook any random Chinese girl for Xu, who was still at the Poxx without me. But logic, during those nocturnal ramblings, didn't have much of a hold on me.

The animal-shaped face creams in the convenience stores reminded me of childhood toys, and I felt a strange pang in my chest as if they'd been stolen from me. I always bought something. Just as a diversion. A pencil, an ugly dragon keychain. When you're down on yourself it's nice to know you can acquire little pieces of the world and

carry them around with you. Even ugly dragon keychains
are part of the world. I paid with my phone, because in
Shanghai cash has all but disappeared. The cashier scanned
the code without smiling.

At night, in the hotel, I looked at myself in the mirror.
My body was pudgy and unremarkable. My body was a
constant thought, except when I slept. In my dreams,
between my head and my feet, I had a shapeless darkness
that sometimes swallowed up its surroundings, like a
black hole. The expressways, plane trees, city buses,
concrete apartment blocks, everything vanished into the
void between my ankles and sternum. At night, in the
hotel, I looked at myself in the mirror. Something didn't
add up: I was in China, halfway across the world, but alas,
I was still me.

"Ruben, since you've been gone, I've put on weight
and moved to China and fallen in love with a girl you
wouldn't like," I said to his picture after Xu wrote me
good night, or didn't, as I switched on the lamp in the
pitch dark, my head awash with dopamine and confusion
and maniacal veneration. And I curled up with my
twin—a little kiss on his forehead, or the blue of his eyes,
where the glass splintered—seeking protection or simply
a thought of something other than Xu.

13

Brain

November 18 was my and Ruben's birthday. I didn't tell Xu. I didn't tell anyone. I decided that it would just be Ruben's birthday. I found an open café, next to a wrought-iron lamppost with a pair of shiny cherubs. I went in and got two croissants, one for me and one for my brother, and wolfed them down standing there, the hot matcha cream dribbling down my chin, staining my coat radioactive green.

I went home, tottering a little. In bed I checked my phone and found messages from Xu. They were in Chinese. It was her way of dominating me. Making herself indecipherable, forcing me to make the effort of comprehension. I opened the dictionary app, then changed my mind and closed it. I cursed her under my breath: *sadist, narcissist.* Cursing to myself was the only time I still used Italian.

It was still Saturday. It was still night. Midnight. My head was spinning. I put my phone on airplane mode and ate the cake I'd gotten at the supermarket before deciding to skip my birthday. Outside the thick glass, a few high-rises switched off, except for the gym where dark shapes of women continued flittering like fish. The offices remained faintly lit, a yellowish and gloomy light which would last until daybreak. It was my first birthday without Ruben, the first on which I was all alone in the world.

The next day was Sunday and we went to Suzhou. A typical Sunday trip. Romantic boat rides on a shimmering river, down ancient canals. Girls playing the flute. Traditional jute jackets sold for cheap. Lion Grove Garden: an incredible labyrinth of rock. Huge waffles that tasted like nothing but were so warm and soft they comforted you to the core. Music. Lots of music. Canals and skies smothered by music. Everything was over the top. Everything should have been amazing. The night before I'd left my psychiatrist in Rome a voice mail, because things had stopped seeming amazing and I wanted to increase my dose of fluoxetine.

We ate lunch at an empty restaurant, all red, served by robot waiters. They didn't look like the Japanese robots from the 2000s, so humanoid as to be disorienting, but the white and boxy ones from the eighties, with big soulless eyes and concentric flashing lights. I said to Xu that Suzhou was interesting because there was so much past and so much future. "The present is missing," she remarked, grabbing the last piece of Peking duck. I didn't understand what she meant. Two beautiful, gaunt young women in Qing-era dress broke into a slow, heartwrenching song, plucking the strings of a zheng.

Back home, I was still hungry. As if I hadn't eaten at all. An astonishing, painful hunger. But the fridge was empty. I turned on the TV. They were advertising IKEA grand openings all over Asia. In the display rooms in Tokyo, they projected a hologram of a girl, a computer-generated influencer. I watched absently. In my head I went over every time Xu had touched me, kissed me, chewed on me. It all seemed like a lifetime ago. It was clear I'd just been one of many. Her Western phase, her exotic summer fuck. I touched myself on the couch, listless and nauseated, as the commercial went on, with the perfect room and the imaginary woman, her imaginary life in a little real room, and I thought of Xu, her beauty and her indifference, and the two concepts mixed together, and as I came my body went numb, like a piece of furniture from the ad, one of those mattresses whole families flop on to test, and I pictured the aisles of IKEA lit up bright as day and the families holding hands and falling back, and my flabby body under all the happy families in the world, for their love to rest on, their real love, the kind I had never had.

14

Eardrums

The days passed quickly, neurotically. December came. Sometimes, while I ate breakfast, I imagined I was talking to Ruben. I told him: *I don't think Xu loves me. Not the way people do on TV. She doesn't give me gifts, she doesn't get all teary-eyed and tell me she's afraid of losing me, and she never talks about a future together. She only talks about her past, and in her past I obviously don't figure. What am I supposed to do, Ruben? What am I supposed to do?*

On the evening of December 5, my psychiatrist called me back while I was at the market, in the fruit section.

"It's too expensive for you to call me here," I told him, and he replied that he wanted to see how I was doing, in a voice rendered warm and soothing by professional routine.

"Do you want to set up a Skype appointment? Tomorrow, at your five P.M.?"

I wondered what his voice sounded like with his mother, with his girlfriend. With a helpless little girl. I said nothing, standing at the fuchsia fruit that looked like human faces. They had tiny green flecks, thin as fingernails, at the points where eyes and noses and mouths would be. A toothless janitor pushed a mop across the floor, wiping up a thick, sticky substance. The psychiatrist asked me again how I was doing, gently breaking into my silence, and I wanted to cry, because it had been so long since anyone had showed me that kind of concern. Then I remembered that showing concern was his job, the way mopping the floor was for the toothless young man. I replied curtly that everything was fine; my message was nothing, just a passing mood. The cleaner left. I hung up. The sticky substance was still there. Now it seemed integrated into the floor. An insidious green hue in the tiles. Under the neon it shone like stained glass on a church in the distance.

On the eighth, it was Immaculate Conception, but there's no Christmas in China. I thought of my Christmases in Rome, the fake China-made trees decorated all over with plastic orbs, Ruben singing "Silent Night" while I tape-recorded him. I thought of those transparent cassettes with black tape. How it'd get caught in the player and you had to stick your pinky finger in the hole to wind it back, your motions careful and apprehensive, for fear of losing the music, the imprinted voice.

That day Xu took me to a cheap hotel next to the insect market. It was late morning, a mild, muggy day. Before finding the entrance, a wide, rusty door, we passed a series of dingy spots set up for cricket-fighting. "Don't go in those places," she told me, looking for the right intercom. I peeked inside. I saw a group of men huddled together in the semidarkness. Xu grabbed my hand and we entered the hotel.

Our room smelled like fried food and there was curly hair on the pillows. Out the windows you could see the tents and stalls with jumpy crickets in cages, gnats in thin plastic boxes with a plastic green disc, a device that enables them to breathe. As she stroked my face, neck, breasts, she told me about cricket fights. They took place in the leafy park just behind where we were, next to the metro, but it was usually closed and people jumped the fence to get in. She told me about the men who participated in these things. Drooly, hunched men, with wide toothless smiles, playing with bugs like they were dolls. You could buy tiny inlaid cases to house the crickets, and delicate porcelain feeding bowls. Regular crickets, vomit-green field crickets. Little pets that have springy legs instead of sweet faces and are so delicate they can be squashed with a finger. They're not much for company, but they remind you of your size, your banal power to kill. And they remind you that you're capable of loving something small and ugly.

After sex we went up a steep staircase to a warehouse with a big market inside. There were long dirty tables covered in objects, some precious treasures, others just old. A silver ashtray with engraved swallows on it. Elegant turn-of-the-century marionettes. Bracelets with tarnished dragon heads. Tin boxes with women pilots, their smiles splintered by the decades. All the vendors slept on reclining chairs. "Want this one? It looks like you," said Xu, picking up a fifties doll with Western features, only one arm, and alien-green eyeballs.

We left the market stalls and headed into the labyrin-thine pet section. Narrow aisles, shielded from the sun. Cats and dogs crammed into cages everywhere, waiting to be chosen, to be loved. Neon orange tadpoles in foil packages. Newborn turtles with Hello Kitty stickers on their shells dinged against each other in a bowl. "Want one?" a woman with lemon-colored teeth asked me. I turned to look for Xu who wasn't there, and my breath caught in my throat.

The next day she took me to Qibao, a suburb west of Shanghai. I realize that I say "she took me" as if I were a package or a child, but that's how it felt. We walked from the metro station down a shabby, unremarkable street, dotted with secondhand stores. The signs over the shops were peeling and faded from their original colors. Inside, anemic light revealed glittery tank tops and sweaters with big, garish flowers. At the end of the street stood the old part of town. A small square with a temple and a thousand little paths intricately radiating out. You had to walk quickly down the narrow alleys so as not to collide with the animalistically advancing crowd. A terrible crowd. People pressed into one another, licking green ice creams or eating glistening fried squid. Straight ahead you saw a horizon made only of heads, a dark sea moving to the rhythm of deafening chatter. To the right, a stream of booths selling all kinds of things. Little wooden balls with dragon carvings, faux jade necklaces, greasy scorpions on skewers. Pork trotters gleaming on racks like diamonds. Legions of ducks, blank-eyed and regal-headed, hung on the walls.

Sitting on a step, away from the crowd, we ate fried roaches on sticks. Her choice. Behind us an old woman in a headscarf was selling black broth.

"You know, right, that Chinese people don't actually eat insects?"

"No, I didn't. So why do you sell them?"

"To appease the tourists. Because that's the image they have of us, and that they want to see confirmed when they come here to see us up close."

"That seems kind of convoluted."

"You don't believe me? Don't you know people say we'll eat anything that moves?"

"Who does?"

"Everyone. Westerners."

"And it's not true?"

"It is. But not insects."

"Well, why are we eating them, then?"

"Because I'm with you and you're a tourist. It's what you want. It's how you want to see me."

"You don't know what I want. Plus I'm not a tourist. Not at all."

"What are you, then?" she said, her mouth full.

"I don't know. I'm a teacher. A person who lives here."

"And what else?"

"What do you mean?"

"What else are you?"

"I'm your girlfriend," I said, immediately regretting it.

"That's not about you. I asked what *you* are."

"I'm a woman. A mammal. An Earth dweller. How's that?"

"I was expecting to hear 'twin.' You haven't brought up your brother in a while."

I felt uneasy. I dumped the skewer in the trash.

"What I am is none of your business," I said.

Xu burst out laughing. She was so beautiful when she laughed that I'd always forget she was laughing at how pathetic I was.

That night she took me to the Wild Insect Museum in Pudong, to gaze at six-foot ocher reptiles and hordes of teeming, buzzing bugs. After the big room with cockroaches in glass cubes and flashy pythons, we went down a narrow hallway with tanks on both sides containing motionless alligators. Their desperation, in such confined spaces, surrounded by synthetic greenery, showed in their deathlike postures.

"Xu, check out this reptile. It looks like something from another world."

"Of course. What you see here are extraordinary creatures. In everyday life we only get the regular ones."

"Like what, lizards?"

"Like the snake you picture when you think of the word *snake*."

"A garter snake."

"Right. It's not especially beautiful or even dangerous. To defend itself it just plays dead, or bares its fangs and pretends to shoot venom. Basically, its aggression is a lie."

"I think it also releases . . ."

"Musk from its anal glands, which smells repulsive. But it doesn't do anything, it's all theater."

"How come you know so much about snakes?"

"Old story . . . When I was little I would run away from home a lot and go to this temple in a nearby village called Jinshan Temple. It had two snakes in a glass cage . . . I'd sit there and watch them. For hours. I'd lose all sense of time, I was entranced. They would twist around each other. It was like they were one. I thought: this is love."

"Why were the snakes there?"

"Because one autumn night, in 2002, the monks saw a white python circling in the water under the imperial bridge in front of the Bailong Cave. It was exactly five feet, six inches long, and had red eyes, a rare type of python, gentle, harmless. They realized it was Bai Suzhen, the white snake that once fell in love with a mortal named Xu Xian and turned into a woman to marry him. But then one day a monk revealed that she wasn't human, revealed her secret."

"I feel like I'm missing something. And how do you know the exact length, all those details?"

"There was a newspaper article about them on the tank. So while I watched the snakes, I'd always read it. I memorized it the way you people memorize your prayers."

"It sounds like a good story."

"Yes, isn't it beautiful? The reincarnation of two lovers who couldn't be together in human form, but eventually got their chance. My aunt would come find me, totally pissed off, and take me home. And my father . . ."

She stared at me, her eyes suddenly vacant.

"My father would beat me, bad. With a belt. He'd make me promise not to run away again."

"Xu . . . I'm sorry."

She jiggled her arm with the jade bracelet.

"That's why this is chipped. One time he threw me against the wall, and the bracelet hit the edge of a cabinet. My mother had given it to me for my birthday. I was thirteen."

"Xu . . . I don't know what to say . . ."

"You don't have to say anything. I'm just telling you what happened. I don't need your sympathy. I don't need sympathy from anyone."

We came to the last room. Outside a bleak gift shop, two motionless llamas gazed out from their enclosure in resignation. I tried to pet one with kind eyes. I wanted to ask Xu about her father, but at the same time I didn't. I was worn out. She was waiting for me impatiently, typing on her phone. I bought some tacky, useless keychains, turning them round and round in my hands during the endless taxi ride to the Poxx.

Since we'd started going to the Poxx more we'd been fucking less. Somehow the Poxx, with its vulgar lights and pounding music, had replaced our intimacy. Xu waved at someone across the room. I couldn't see her face, just a blurry composite of features. I leaned against the bar and ordered my usual sake. I downed it in one gulp. I looked around, my head empty. The vintage signs on the walls, replicas of American road signs and English tea brands and motivational sayings, indiscriminately mixed, looked aggressive. Their lack of coherence was aggressive. Their lack of narrative. ROUTE 66, TWININGS TEA AND COFFEE MERCHANTS, LIVE LAUGH LOVE, WORK HARD AND BE NICE, THIS IS OUR HAPPY PLACE. I went outside to get some air while Xu chatted with random people. In the bruise-dark alley, a woman sitting on a red towel motioned for me to come over. I obeyed. She was emaciated, her sparse hair mousy brown. Her opaque stare was like a wall, something separating her from life. She looked at me and said, in English: "Let me get a good look at your face." I blushed. I leaned closer. She smelled of alcohol and urine. "You have a little wrinkle on your nose"—and then—"you were born with it and can't do anything about it, but it is the obstacle to your happiness." I felt like laughing but instead I burst out crying. She asked me for twenty yuan.

That night Xu slept over. It was the first time and she didn't like my room. She said she felt suffocated. She paced between the bed and the kitchenette, and she examined my notebooks and pens, my leather bags, burnt pans, silver necklaces, with a perplexed and anxious expression. We ordered fried frog legs and fell asleep in front of the TV with takeout boxes strewn across the floor. Late in the night she woke up with a start, screaming. I switched on the lamp and saw her shaking, her forehead glistening with sweat.

"Xu, everything's OK. What were you dreaming about?"

"Nothing, it doesn't matter."

"What do you mean, it doesn't matter?"

"Do you have anything to drink? Vodka?"

"No. I never drink at home."

"Fuck that. I'm going out."

"No. Wait. Come here."

I tried to hold her. She wriggled out of my arms. She was still trembling. She made an abrupt lunge for her phone and knocked over the framed picture of me and Ruben.

I ran to pick it up, my heart in my throat.

It wasn't broken.

There was the usual, lone crack, like a fallen hair. Standing there, holding my brother and myself, I looked at Xu, who was taking deep breaths, trying to calm down.

"Now will you tell me what your dream was about?"

"Stop asking. It's not important. It's normal to have nightmares when you live in Shanghai. This city gets into your head."

15

Vertebrae

When I woke up the sky was deep blue and Xu had disappeared. She had remade the bed perfectly. Even the pillow had no indentation, as if it hadn't supported the weight of her head for hours. I pressed my nose into the fabric to inhale the last traces of her mysterious, spicy scent. I took off my clothes. I tried not to look at myself in the mirror. In the shower I masturbated, frenetically, to extinguish my anxiety the way you would a fire.

I went to work. The short walk to the school seemed endless. I was tired, my legs felt heavy, the medicinal blue sky bothered my eyes. And there was construction everywhere: men toiling, breathing hard, busy repairing, demolishing. Up on ladders and cranes, metal scaffolds, in the sun, pale sweat-beaded faces focused on some imperceptible detail. I stepped around a sinkhole. Everyone walked briskly with calm and purposeful expressions, entering and exiting the metro like ants in and out of an anthill. Didn't they realize what was happening? Didn't they notice all that fervor and destruction? Didn't it frighten them that soil and cement crumble so easily? And that, with the same ease and speed, could be put back together as if they'd never collapsed? My head was spinning. I went toward Jing'an Park. The square to the right, the one on the cover of my Shanghai travel guide, was gone: in its place was a huge pit full of workers and rubble. I peeked through the gate to look at the crater and rocks and the dusty commotion of the cranes. The only time I'd cracked that guide was on the plane, at some point in the night, my Italian night which outside the window was already Chinese and strewn with puffy clouds. Of the square, it said: *The perfect spot to stop for a break.*

During class I kept checking my phone, hoping Xu would write me, but I forced myself not to write her. I had to leave her her space. That's what you do in relationships. You respect the other person's silence by offering the gift of additional silence, making sure that the sum total of silence isn't so great as to cancel everything out. Silence has to be doled out carefully. Like hydrogen peroxide on a cut. It seems harmless, it disinfects, makes a snowy white foam on a splotch of blood. But it drains the color out of anything that soaks in it for too long.

As I explained to my students the difference between *la mia casa* and *casa mia*, Xu's nightmare popped into my head and I couldn't get it out. Mechanically I reviewed grammar all the while picturing on the orange wall the image of Xu, shaking like she'd been in a shipwreck, covered in sweat after emerging from a violent ocean of feeling. I hated that she didn't want to tell me anything. I hated that she shared with me only the shell of her inner life, keeping the volatile core to herself. Everything I knew about her had been recounted in a cold, anecdotal manner, as if talking about a film. She told me only the things that over time had become inert. But I was hungry for what was drowning her still. I wrote her a message: *I'm sorry we fought. I care about you and I just want us to be happy.* She didn't reply.

That night I sat glued to the window gazing at the high-rises. It calmed me. I tried to memorize the order in which the lights went off. I followed the silhouettes of women finishing aerobics classes and disappearing into locker rooms, then spotted them later exiting from the ground floor and watched them until they turned toward the metro. I'd picked up a packaged dinner at the market, cold ramen with chicken, but I left it in its plastic on the table. My stomach was in knots. I drank some cheap wine and spent the rest of the night in the armchair with my headphones on, binging *The Could've-Gone-All-the-Way Committee*. It was a Japanese show that made no sense. A committee would listen to a person tell them about a past circumstance in which they missed a romantic opportunity. Not making a move on someone, not having slept with someone, things like that. Then the committee deliberated whether, given the evidence, the situation could have turned out differently. The contestants found comfort in knowing that yes, things could have gone differently, if only they'd been more attentive, more sensitive, more clever, better at life.

Xu didn't answer my calls for days. In class, I tried to focus on my students. On the importance of helping them to express themselves in another language. Every language brings new emotions along with it. What had Chinese brought me? Love, hate, frustration, solitude. Was my solitude in Chinese lesser or greater than my solitude in Italian? And love, what kind of love was it? And something else too. A feeling without a name, a feeling of being small, like being three years old again and needing to be held more than anything. It wasn't quite love, because it was impersonal. It's not love when a baby animal at the zoo clings to a plush mother. It wasn't even solitude, because companionship didn't slake it, only reinforced it. It was an obscure hunger, so full of ferocity and hope it seemed religious. Absolute like our first cry when we're pushed out of the uterus, forced to enter the world.

During break I went to the café in the school building. I'd never been. I was about to order a coffee, but the barista, her enormous eyes in sapphire blue contacts, pointed to my phone. I went on their website and ordered an espresso, the screen said it would be ready at 11:41. While I waited, I struck up a conversation in Chinese with a colleague I knew a little. She was standing there to my right. It worked for a few minutes. The conversation was basic and I was able to sustain it. Then it took a slightly complex turn. I couldn't follow. Meaning evaporated. My coffee came. My hand trembled a little on the plastic cup. She asked me, maybe, if I had made any friends. I didn't know how to answer. I didn't even know whether I had understood. Understood her words. Understood my life. Was Xu a friend? An enemy?

I waved goodbye and left. I walked down the crowded halls, my head down, immersed in my confusion. It was a confusion without words, in no language. And Chinese is an invertebrate language, like a snake. It lacks the backbone of conjugations. The grammatical difference between doing something and already having done it, between past, present, and future, is located outside the verb. It's a prosthesis, a particle to append at will. Time is a detail to relate only when absolutely necessary. The syntax doesn't require it. In short, in Chinese, there's no difference between "Ruben is my brother" and "Ruben was my brother." Between "Xu loves me" and "Xu used to love me," for a while, at certain moments, in her room or out in the city, on the asphalt, on a hard bed in a high-rise hotel.

16

Lips

She resurfaced the following Thursday, texting me to meet her at the Poxx. By that point the Poxx felt like a grave. The act of descending those endless, dark granite stairs with the fuchsia neon sign like that of a roadside motel, and my increasingly lugubrious moods. One morning I caught a glimpse of the place from a bookstore in a tall building nearby: the staircase, seen from above, reminded me of the inside of a broken bone. And there were too many voices all mixed up, and the tables were too close together. Touching them left a greasy film on your fingers for hours afterward.

When I got there, Kelly/Biyu/Angélie was telling Xu about a German musician she was sleeping with who didn't treat her well. It was ten. Then eleven. Rows of Westerners guffawed at other tables, spearing their food with forks like weapons of a more authoritative civilization. I'd learned to recognize the type. Dumb Europeans with a blind and predatory love for China, who want to fuck Chinese people or adopt Chinese babies, wake up looking at Chinese eyes and Chinese skin. They exclusively frequented Western-influenced locales, with lots of greenery and lounge music and plastic Buddha statues. They went to the Poxx, which was a no-man's-land, neutral and artificial as a studio set. I despised them even more than Xu's friends. Kelly/etc. whined on against the wall of vintage license plates, against the silence, turning snappy, serious, electric with anger. Unrequited love has an astonishing energetic charge.

At a certain point Xu rubbed her cheek and said "He doesn't deserve you" and similar clichés, but then some smart and motherly things, things that lit up Kelly's pale, symmetrical face, like "I can't tell you to dump him, if you're with him it's because your subconscious is compelled to reenact some ugly childhood scenario, but listen, I care about you, and I wish I could keep you from seeing him, like I would with a sister." With me she had never been so transparent, so considerate. With me she was opaque and selfish. Now Kelly was visibly better, smiling, drying her tears, letting down her canary-yellow hair in a gesture of relief and relaxation. I couldn't remember the last time I felt better after talking, or after someone had talked to me. Maybe no one, for ages, had spoken to me with kindness. Maybe I didn't to myself either. I touched my mouth and it felt like a relic.

We exchanged greetings. I went to one side and they to the other. I couldn't tell whether Kelly was pretty or not, because whenever I saw her I maniacally isolated each part of her face. Small eyes, small nose, thin and pale lips. I separated all the parts and then didn't know how to put them together. But that night I noticed she had a pink sore at the corner of her mouth. Which had nothing to do with Xu, just her immune system, and it shouldn't have bothered me. But on the way back to my hotel, with cold legs and a broken umbrella, I imagined them in the metro talking about it, heads pressed together, rattling on about fevers and vitamin deficiencies as if conversing about debilitated organisms had something to do with going back home to a safe and secure place, and Xu came so close to that red bump, the proximity between Kelly's sick lips and hers was alarming. Xu said: "You need to take better care of yourself." Or: "I know a cream that'll work wonders." Things like that. Little things. But once I started imagining them, I couldn't stop. Their bodies swaying on the speeding train, then the stop, the goodbye, their faces grazing for an instant, the threat of infection passing between them. In that vortex of obsessive thoughts even the virus that had settled next to Kelly's mouth seemed like a sign of love: the organism, languid and helpless, yielding to the graft, a pustule blossoming at the corner of the mouth like a flower.

That night I couldn't sleep. I got up. It was four. In pajamas and a sweatshirt of Ruben's I ran all the way to the metro. I stopped to catch my breath next to the construction site, feeling the cold enter my throat and my body ignite with panic. There was a sign saying something in Chinese I wasn't lucid enough to understand. Underneath, the completely incorrect English translation said: SLIP AND FALL WITH CARE.

I reached Xu's. From the sidewalk, I observed the row of lighted windows. Kitchens full of food but no people, empty living rooms with big TVs flashing blue. Her window was too high, inscrutable. I stared at the bright light, so close to the moon, shivering in my thin clothes. I wondered what Ruben would have thought if he could see me at that moment, standing in the cold, in his small, slightly warped sweatshirt, desperation undoubtedly written all over my face. I wondered that often. But less and less. The more distant his death in time, the less pressing his life was in my mind. This both comforted me and made me feel alone.

After about ten minutes I thought I saw a dark shape in the window. It was just an instant. Impossible to tell whether it was Xu or a mass that included Xu and Kelly. I waited for a sign. A face looking out, the yellow flash of Kelly's long hair: that acid, alarm-yellow, like police tape. Maybe Kelly's name wasn't really Biyu. Maybe there existed an even more intimate name, a name she gave only to girls she was sleeping with. Maybe Xu said it under her breath, in bed, as she rested her head on her lap. I thought of how Egyptian gods had a name they never revealed because it would grant too much power to anyone who knew it. When Ra was poisoned by a snake that Isis created out of his own saliva, the only way to save himself was to reveal his secret name to her.

I summoned my nerve. I rang the buzzer. She answered immediately. "It's me," I said in an anxious whisper. I ran up. She was alone. She was studying at the table, eating dried mango. Relief burst from my head like an exorcism. She came up to me and we kissed against the wall. I cupped her cheeks with my cold, shaky hands. I felt my zeal clash with her calm.

"Xu, bite my lip. As hard as you can."

"I don't feel like it."

She was tired, her head was somewhere else. The alien egg lit up in a thousand colors, out there, out of nowhere.

"You don't care about me."

"Why do you say that?"

"You're always with your friends."

"I've known them for longer."

My heart stopped.

"But . . . you and me . . ."

"What is it you want to tell me? Be clear."

"You're not in love with me."

She looked at me, perplexed and amused. She always looked at me perplexed and amused. When I spoke, when I was silent, when I stuck my tongue down her throat. I was a zoo to her, an assembly of exotic animals to gawk at.

"Answer me, Xu."

"It wasn't a question. It was a statement."

"And you have nothing to say?"

"First I'd like you to calm down."

"I hate you," I said, immediately regretting it.

I knew very well that past a certain pain threshold, words regress, lose communicative value, serve only to release tension, like the crying of newborns.

"No . . . It's not true that I hate you . . . It's that . . ."

Xu sighed, a bored look in her eyes, and the room quivered a little, like reality before a breakdown.

This wasn't me. I was a rational person. I always had been. I had a job that required mental control. But this feeling for Xu took me to a wild and hostile place in my mind, where logic struggled to take root, and when it did every thought came up twisted, humid, rotted.

"You hate me, you love me, you're a disaster. What am I supposed to do with a girl like you?" she said, running her fingers through her hair. I burst into tears. I hadn't cried for seven months. Since the day of the funeral. Love is a lot like a funeral. The surrender, all the ritual. I kept crying and she kept looking at me blankly like a Jean-Paul Laurens portrait. Her blankness aggravated my crying, which became loud and aggressive like a child's. I covered my eyes. Behind my hands I imagined her standing there motionless and curious, an anthropologist of my sadness.

"Bite me, please," I said. I was ashamed of having become so pathetic and needy, but I thought it was the only way to truly bond with another person. She bit my lip hard, violently. I felt the teeth sink in and then release the benumbed flesh. She bit me again, harder. I ran to the bathroom and looked in the mirror. My lip swelled, contorting my face into a strange grimace. A grimace that corresponded to no emotion. I spent the night. I didn't want to leave, no matter what.

17

Tongues

The next morning we sat at the table littered with magazines and lipsticks drinking green tea. They don't strain tea in China, and the bottoms of our cups contained a clump of foliage that expanded gently in the boiling water. Then I lay back on the couch to play Candy Crush. I spent two hours matching identically colored candies. Xu was off by herself, studying a little and chatting with who knows who. She turned on the TV, which said BEWARE OF PM2.5 PARTICLES. I was happy when I understood an entire sentence in Chinese: it was the mystery that was my distance from Xu slowly dwindling, bringing her closer to me. A mystery made of monosyllables, retroflex consonants, *H* sounds like wind on the highway. But at that moment, the TV phrase left me indifferent. Xu turned and asked if pork tongue was okay for lunch. And green beans with shrimp sauce. I thought of how all the food Ruben cooked was affectionate: warm, soft on the tongue. There were no animals, just delicate leaves, soothing sauces. The only exception was his salmon tart, which he made because my parents were crazy about it. Xu asked me again about the pork tongue. I said, "I don't know." I said, "Whatever is fine." I was tired of having to think of what I wanted.

I was angry. I was angry and wished I was angrier. That the anger went deeper. I hated that my love for Xu softened my anger toward her. On my phone dictionary I looked up how to say *fuck* in Chinese. No. Something more specific. *Vagina.* I wanted to ask her if she had seen Kelly's vagina. I imagined it like a rotting fruit, soft and languid, like ones in the countryside left on the ground to turn to mush. I imagined Xu's fingers exploring that dark pulp with a mix of desire and disgust. I found *vagina* in the dictionary: it was *yindao.* Literally, "dark path," like Dante's "via oscura." Obscure. Or "hidden, shadowy," each synonym more elegant than the last, each further away from an actual vagina, transforming anatomy into something abstract, almost religious. A path can be monastic or self-destructive, for addicts or ascetics. Something that had to be followed by abnegation. I wanted to follow Xu into the dark and damp core of her being.

Which isn't just her cunt. It's the dark path to which her cunt is the entrance: it's a humble pilgrimage toward her head. Undertaken like a mystic, arrogant and self-sacrificing. These thoughts provoked a mix of arousal and spite. Maybe that's just how desire is. I dropped the phone on the couch, my heart racing, and went over to Xu. I snatched the pink phone from her hands. Everything outside was gray, coated with smog, but there was sun too, a weak sun that peeked through the gray, creating little fissures of light. *Dark path.* The Chinese language is so metaphorical that the only way to be direct is to be silent. To wound. Act on the body with an unequivocal gesture. I took off my floral blouse and grabbed her head. I pressed it into my breasts. There was no need to speak. She, submissive and fierce, bit me hard.

"Did you fuck Kelly?"

"When?"

She turned to me. We were lying naked on the couch; with headaches after fucking for so long.

"When? Yesterday. Any other day. You tell me. Are you fucking Kelly?"

"You're too much. You suffocate me," she said, and went to the mirror to brush her hair.

"Please," I said to her back, my voice tiny like an insect's. A chirping roach on a gigantic sidewalk. I buried my face in my hands.

Seven months ago I'd lost my faith in words. When Ruben died and I hadn't said anything meaningful to him. When he died and hadn't said anything meaningful to me. Yet I fall in love and return to that pathetic, desperate faith in language. Like any other, faith in words can neither be verified nor disproved. Like any faith, it can make you into a martyr.

"Just Kelly or are there others? Do you still fuck your exes, the ones in the pictures?"

"Why do you want to know?"

"Because it's the truth, Xu."

"The way you say my name makes me laugh."

"Don't change the subject. Tell me the truth."

"The truth is boring."

"No, the truth is important."

"Why do you need to know?"

"Because. Because I need to."

"You're not a little girl, and I'm not your mother, it's not my duty to fulfill your needs."

A wave of nausea hit me and I locked myself in the bathroom. As I retched I heard the sound of channel surfing, the programs changing and the volume rising, the squawking of cartoons and commercials, fake, split-second emotions, simulated desires, then ten minutes of shrill soap opera voices interspersed with cars speeding into the wind, flat piano music, raucous laughter. She called me when the pork tongue came.

18

Fat

Love deposits all over the body, like fat. There are those who gain weight in their backside and those in their middle. There are those who gain in their faces until their features are so stretched they're unrecognizable even to themselves. The same goes for love. It settles in the parts of the body that best tolerate weight and transfiguration. It can be felt in throbbing temples or tingling fingertips—a commotion like a swarm, insects scurrying in the dark—or in the sweaty nook of a knee. The eyes get red and itchy. The stomach burns. The nerves pull in the elbow like worn strings on an old violin. Love burns the cheeks and the earlobes, which turn the morbid color of crushed roses in a notebook. The ovaries ache; the nipples assume a bovine consistency. Once love pounds in the chest it has already spread to the entire body: it must be released through the genitals, and if any remains, a cut must be made at the precise point of the blockage so it can bleed out.

19

Cheek

The next day, she disappeared. Again. She stopped responding to calls and texts. I knew she was punishing me for my little rebellion and I was furious with myself. Furious for having asked something of her, for expecting her to deem me worthy of attention. After school, in the harsh bathroom light, I repeated her name in the mirror. *Xu. Xu. Xu. Xu Xu Xu Xu Xu. Xu Xu Xu Xu Xu Xu Xu Xu Xu Xu Xu Xu* until it was just tongue against palate. A deranged trail of human speech. And only then, when it had lost all meaning, when all I had in my mouth was an *X* and a vowel, a sibyl like a snake's hiss, did I realize: I had loved alone, all alone, like a dog. I'd tossed my love out like a boomerang without making sure it came back.

That night I stationed myself in front of her house, buzzing her intercom continuously. No response. I even stayed through the rain. Unmoving, waiting, under a garbage-colored sky. I tried again three days later, in vain. I inquired with the other Italian teacher, Rosa: Xu had stopped coming to class. I caught a cold; I recovered. A few weeks went by. I went to work but I checked my phone constantly under my desk, or hid out in the bathroom to call her over and over, on the toilet, until my sacrum was sore. It was December 20. My students saw me distraught, distracted, pale. They asked me how I was, they wished me Merry Christmas. I played along as if I found some sense in it: *Merry Christmas to you too.* But it made no sense for anyone: neither for them, who don't celebrate Christmas, nor for me, who had nothing to celebrate.

I fell back into the habit of thinking about my brother all day. Like before Xu. I thought about the pumpkin ginger tarts he made before he got sick. The wasabi beet soup, the quinoa-stuffed zucchini flowers. He was in his second year of culinary school, studying Chinese, too, and starting to dream of his restaurant in Shanghai. I'd never asked him why Shanghai. Where the idea had come from. That strange, remote dream. A book, a movie, a documentary? After he died, I tried, compulsively, to make his salmon tart. Three, four, five attempts. Something was always missing, a subtle, sweet aftertaste I couldn't re-create. I didn't have the heart to throw it out, but not to eat it either. I'd throw the spoon against the wall, frustrated, then sit for hours watching the salmon darken, dry out, start to give off a sharp smell, until my parents yelled for me to get rid of it.

No sign of Christmas on the Chinese streets. It was an end to December outside of time. I ate supermarket food in my hotel. On Christmas Eve morning a sales-person with a sample tray slapped me in the face when I took one: I was supposed to wait to be served with the proper utensil. "I didn't know," I whispered, humiliated. I went out into the cold with my cheek burning.

In the afternoons I roamed titanic shopping malls presided over by vinyl statues of comic book characters. From the clothing stores on the first floor to the statio-nery and toy stores on the middle floors, to the gourmet restaurants on top. I went round and round, each time noting different items, as if in a maze looking for the way out. Violent, yellow lighting, anime girls crying fat tears on gaudy pullovers. In the housewares store, dustpans with plastic crocodile handles and a shocking-pink doormat that said: YOU MUST STAY UNTIL THE END.

I went out every night. In the little eateries behind the temple, I sat in dim light surrounded by old people, eating frenetically and spitting little bones on the table, slurping my pungent brown soup, scooping tiny bird limbs and slimy black mushrooms from the bottom. At the back of the foreigners' bar, behind the massive meringue-colored fifty-thousand-dollar-a-night hotel, I drank far more sake than my medication allowed.

Sometimes, drunk, I walked over to the Poxx without going in. I peeked down the stairway from above and kept walking. The streets of the Luwan District blurred. The sky bled into the enormous sidewalks glistening with rain, the renovated French-style mansions. Dull cherry-wood facades, frosty museum-like windows, houses from the twenties for rich people and political figureheads. Vomit crept up my throat and everything was faded like a once-known place that your memory has abandoned. People saw me tottering and called out to me in the street, shadowy faces breaking into smiles, and I looked away because I couldn't tell if it was kindness or pity.

I spent New Year's Eve walking around the district for hours, all the way to Nanjing Road. A burst of contrasting light and color exploded in the darkness. Flashing signs overlapped. At a kiosk on the sidewalk a chubby girl in a Minnie Mouse costume was selling candy. Behind her stood a giant statue of Molly, the rubber doll sold in vending machines all over the city. Young sweethearts hovered over the machines pressing buttons and trying to guess which one would come out.

It used to be the red light district. With cheap hookers and imported food. Scrawny kids sold to the factories, who worked fourteen hours a day then dropped dead on their way home, like pigeons, on a streetcorner dirty with piss and animal parts. Then there were the unwanted, the children of wayward desire, remainders of a voracious, futureless love, born in an abyss of hunger and poverty and drowned in the drainage canals: from 1920 to 1940, twenty-nine thousand such bodies were found. When the toy-women with round rosy faces came out of the 668 brothels in the quarter like black shadows in dark alleys, huddled and flailing like shoals of fish, while everything screamed or moaned—because the noises of living can sound like cries for help—careful to step over the children's bodies, their skin yellow-gray, their teeth glossy like quartz.

They say twins are internally linked, and their brains light up in unison like lights on Christmas trees, but it wasn't like that with me and Ruben. I had no advance intimation of his death. Not the day, not the time. I didn't foresee his first timid kiss in a little street behind Piazza Navona, nor his desire to go to China, nor his resignation at realizing he was sick and would never be able to go. My love for him gave me no information about what he felt or how much time he had left. It was an opaque love. It just happened one morning, I was brushing my teeth in his bathroom and he died. He died while I was brushing my teeth. Vigorously, because I had cookie stuck in my back teeth. I had planned to kiss him as he was dying, a little kiss on his eyes, to keep his soul inside me: an Ancient Roman practice. Instead he died as I turned on the faucet, just a few feet away, looking at myself in the mirror. There was a fly on the glass, beating its wings. The nurses made up the room and, in that opacity, we all left the clinic.

I came to a building, something like a mausoleum. I had read about it in my guide, but couldn't remember what it was for. A thousand meters of sparkling white suffocating the black sky. Just outside, a motionless woman in a wheelchair turned her one marble eye on me, unseeing.

20

Throat

On the morning of January 3, Xu reappeared. A text while I was in the shower. I grabbed the phone, dripping wet. *2:30 in front of your place. I'm taking you somewhere.* This time we would meet during the day. I wondered fretfully whether this meant a change of tone in our relationship.

Two hours later she was at the door. She was wearing an emphatic purple dress with puffy sleeves. We hailed a taxi; she gave the driver instructions, instructions full of nasal consonants. When Xu spoke quickly I understood nothing at all, and in my head her words meant whatever I wanted. An address became a compliment, a command to turn right a declaration of love. *This is my girlfriend, isn't she gorgeous?* she said that afternoon, I'd decided. I smiled at her, smiled at the sentence she hadn't said, the Western districts fading into a drab suburb.

The car came to a halt. A woman looked down at us dourly from behind a wall of faded undershirts on a balcony. I recognized the river, gray and motionless as a parking garage. In front was a huge warehouse. We went inside. An expanse of old, rotting wood, rickety beams, and spidery light that shone through the partly barred windows.

"This used to be a textile factory. Then it became a department store, then the headquarters for a religious group that made up mantras to use during nervous break-downs. Then some kind of stockyard. But the animals died. For a while it was full of skulls and spines. And that's it, now it's not anything. At some point every place in Shanghai turns into something else. Then something else again. Then again and again, until they're not anything anymore."

"I noticed."

"A city where things change all the time is dangerous."

"In what sense?"

"You can't rely on it. You can't relax. Do you like this place?"

"I don't know."

"What do you mean you don't know?"

She had bags under her eyes. What had she done the night before, and the one before that? The question caught in my throat.

She undressed me, slowly. My blue sweater, once Ruben's. My tight skirt. Her fingers, small and white like larvas, unbuttoned me lazily. I closed my eyes in the weak winter sun filtering in through a slit in the wall. Xu went on talking about places that became other places. Places that end up carcasses. Ruins. Symbols. Her words were drawn out and velvety; they came from a place halfway toward sleep, a place where emotions only echo the remnants of previous emotions, so when she finished undressing me and said "I love you," I knew full well it wasn't for me, it was a line for someone else or from someone else, impersonal like the stinging glare on your retina after looking into a bright light. I turned away, my arms pressed to my bare sides.

"What are you doing? Turn around."

I turned and only then did I see the others.

Dark shapes were moving frenetically across the room. Their movements were brusque, serpentine. They were fucking, kissing dispassionately. How had I not noticed them before? Was my desire for Xu so strong as to block out everything else? From where I stood they appeared hazy, dimly lit by the streetlight filtering in through the windows. Geometric, impassive bodies. Impervious to love. Every now and then a guttural laugh cut through the silence, and an embrace broke apart. A dark body, in the corner, was doubled over, in tears. Another body, under the stairs, shrank into itself like a worm, its sex balled up between its legs.

"Who are these people?"

"Relax. People like us."

"In what sense?"

"People who don't know where to go. People who aren't at peace with themselves."

"They seem like they're on drugs."

"It's just the yellow pill. I'll explain later. Let's find a more secluded spot."

"No, I don't like this place," I said.

It was like the first day of preschool: alone and confused by the presence of all these others, the sudden awareness of having to coexist with people. I wanted to be with Xu, just Xu, I wanted her to want that too. She laughed. She was laughing at me. Her teeth were granite: a gravestone with no engraving.

She tugged my hand and led me to a corner under an iron staircase. She had me lie down. I could smell the dust and something more elegant, like an expensive perfume that had spilled somewhere. "Now do what I say."

What if my sadness, the sadness I attribute for the sake of convenience to the loss of my brother, were actually an older sadness, a habit of feeling like I exist for the use and consumption of others?

I experienced what followed as if it were an episode of one of my TV shows. As if its meaning could only be made intelligible through a particular convergence of lighting, dialogue, framing, backstory. I closed my eyes. If it really were a TV show, I would have had to take some kind of action. To move the story forward. This is what characters do. They act. They have control. But I didn't act. I didn't control anything. I had completely surrendered to Xu. Her mouth. Her hands. I existed only for her. Her teeth that glinted in the grim light. Those teeth like those of a fantasy monster, any monster, made legendary by a simple, depressing fairy tale: my life, my life without my brother.

Her fingers were cold and precise. They unhooked my new bra, unicorns on blue, and squeezed my breasts. Her every gesture, even erotic, was peremptory, like the movements of a police officer. I wanted to ask her more about the factory, but every time I went to speak, airy, celebratory brass music, blared outside. Then it stopped. Then it started back up again. Louder and louder, like a cruel joke. We lay down on the pavement, naked.

I couldn't believe that Xu had chosen me. Me, someone as hungry for attention as a dog. Any kind of attention. Sappy, compassionate, cruel. I've always been that way. Take the leash, tug on my neck a little more, and my devotion to you will only grow. Once, when I was nine, Ruben's friends came over to play on the PlayStation and were asking me about my favorite games, and I was so flattered by that flow of questions directed at me that rather than interrupt it, I held my pee until I wet myself.

We fucked for hours, Xu and I. We took breaks to eat beef jerky and drink lychee juice. Outside, through the transom windows, the smog-yellow sky seemed not to register the transition from day to night. Everything that once happened in the outside world now happened inside of us. Now and then we were distracted by a splinter poking our skin. Sharp voices outside collided like the sound of breaking glass. A car horn. Things reminding us that beyond our skin there was a world: a clamoring thing that demanded our attention and that would punish us if we didn't listen to it.

Night fell and we became shadows. Xu went skipping to turn on the fluorescent lights. The crumbling warehouse turned uniform yellow like a preschooler's drawing. I was tired, all those hours of joy and of feeling my body, mine and another's. But she was still full of energy; she had bright eyes and an irrepressible smile.

She emptied her purse and out came tubes of lipstick and jars of face cream and an electronic dictionary and finally a glittery pink dildo: a silicone apparatus the color of Barbie guts. Under that mortuary neon it radiated a grotesque cheer. A fluorescent energy. We didn't need a dildo. I told her, "Leave it." She didn't listen. She put it on, her expression serious. She buckled the strap. The music resumed outside. Frivolous, dreamy, the obsessive reiteration of a blissful mood.

"You know, from the age of four I was raised by my grandma. She wasn't mean, but she didn't love me. She preferred my cousin, Ling. Everybody did. Ling was prettier and she was supposed to be the only girl."

"She couldn't have been prettier than you."

"Oh, she was, believe me. Everyone gravitated toward her and complimented her. When my aunt gave me a dress for Christmas, all pink lace, Ling burst out crying, because she was supposed to be the only pretty one."

"That's ridiculous."

". . . And so my grandma took me by the arm and dragged me into my room. I remember it was really dark out. It'd been raining for days, so many days that the garden had turned into a swamp . . . dead leaves blew through my little bedroom window . . . the glass was all dirty . . . My ugly little room, all dirty . . . I remember like it was yesterday . . ."

She towered over me, her eyes half-closed, a dark silhouette with a candy-color dick.

". . . I remember how dark it was and her eyes were even darker. I've never seen eyes like that, Ruben, I swear . . . Then she took a pair of scissors, and . . . she cut the dress into little pieces."

Her voice had suddenly turned petulant and aggressive, like a little girl holding back tears.

"I'm sorry," I said.

"Shhh. I don't want sympathy. I'm just taking care of things."

Her eyes glistening, she kneeled next to me. Completely naked, I was starting to get cold.

"What things?"

"All the things. The holes. The holes, silly."

"The holes?"

"The holes for the nails that love hangs on. You're shaking. Hold on."

She bent over me, against the light, a Mattel plastic alien. Her wide mouth, her sharp shoulders, her little milky breasts. In place of her genitals, a hot pink gummy. She laughed the way you laugh on an empty street at night. Then she took my head and pulled it between her legs. By then it was almost morning; there was no sound. I wanted to go back home and watch TV until I was numb and fell asleep to colorless dreams.

Gripping my head, she bit my ear. A little too hard. I felt a drop of blood fall into my auricle with a tiny plop that touched and frightened me. And then another. "It's going to be okay," Xu said, her voice stark, like that of a little girl accustomed to being alone. My lips closed over the glittering penis.

21

Wrist

For days I was so dominated by that night at the textile factory, by that strange mixture of physical joy and mental fog, that I thought of nothing else. Her stern face, her silicone dick, the detailed story about her grand-mother. I could see the kitchen shears, the sturdy blades glinting in the autumn sun as the old woman sneered and tore into the cloth. As if I had actually seen it. It was a memory of Xu's, but it had become mine. Something that happens when you love too much.

The nights after that we talked on the phone. She had a cold and didn't feel like going out or having me over. We sent each other hundreds of cat videos. There was so much affection between us, tucked under the ferocity, really I had no reason to worry. She might not be exclusive, but she would never actually hurt me. Never. So I told myself. And I believed it. But love obscures details. It makes your gaze generic. It censors signs of approaching danger.

One afternoon she gave me a book of photography by Zhang Lanpo. Incredible shots of tiny fetuses, in black and white, cradled by big skeletons in leafy alcoves. Burnt faces with bloated eyelids and a mournful joy. We were at Jing'an Park, surrounded by surreal sculptures. I set the book on a bench and we took a selfie under an enormous metal bucket suspended in the air, out of which came a cascade of little buckets.

She took me to another, smaller factory, near M50, another, repurposed site. Fucking in rubble, in places that had been other places and then other places and then ceased to be anything, was incredible. Lying in the dust, my head was as empty and light as a plastic cup, like the colored ones for kids. When we were little Ruben and I used cups like that, sniffing at the bitter taste of water in plastic, but we still wanted them for the bright colors. Children fixate on form and disregard substance. Xu smiled as she took off my clothes and laid my head on the step. She opened her mouth and started tasting me.

Love shouldn't create desensitized scars, shinier and rougher than regular skin. At most, shallow wounds that heal quickly. Like the kind you get falling off the swings when you're little, when you launch into the sky, legs outstretched, but the sky pushes you down. Love isn't supposed to hurt. At least, according to TV. On TV, a doomed relationship might warrant slower scenes, with dark, dramatic music to suggest the characters' thoughts, but transition as quickly as possible to other situations. When I opened my eyes again, Xu was inside me. She was part of my body. Flesh in flesh. An infiltration. She moaned impatiently. I dug my nails into her back and her short sweaty hair slipped into my mouth like leeches.

After sex, still sweaty, we went to look at the art. Dozens of galleries in decrepit buildings, stairs that led to locked rooms and blind alleys. Women with bold expressions painted on the walls, long red hair fanning in the wind like flames. A closed store with faceless mannequins in the window, dressed in elegant qipaos, their arms raised as if calling for help. In the last gallery there were ancient Chinese paintings superimposed with holograms of blue-haired women walking on skyscrapers or gazing into the distance, hypnotized by something, vacant. I looked down at my wrist to check the time, but I hadn't been wearing my watch for over a month, and in its place was the glistening, feral imprint of Xu's teeth. A little ideogram that conveyed nothing. A guy at the ticket counter saw my wrist and said, "Hey, you're bleeding."

On January 27, in the course of a day, winter came. The sky turned dirty white and the wind blew cold. The front page of the paper displayed a photo of flying silver carp. A wall of fish, huddled together and ink-shiny, leaping out of the water into a big net waiting to catch them. Another shot pictured smiling tourists, phones in hand, excited by that moment of vitality on the brink of annihilation. It was an article about Qiandao fish soup. *It's a farm-raised silver carp commonly used in China for soup due to its particularly large head, which can weigh up to nine pounds. It is made with tofu, bamboo, coriander, and ham. If tourists can get past the fish head with bulging eyes staring out from the milky broth, they'll discover a true delicacy.*

That night I fell asleep on the couch and woke up to a message from her. It said *526*. And then, *25873*. I studied the numbers on the screen, puzzled. Every time I got closer to Xu she would put another screen between us, something else I had to decipher. I replied *?* and she, *58*. I looked on the internet and found that young Chinese people often use numbers to substitute phrases with similar sounds. They call it Martian language, but it expresses the most basic things in earthly human experience. *526*: I'm hungry. *58*: good night. *25873*: love me until death.

The Saturday after that, we ate at a hole-in-the-wall near my hotel. We slurped up dark broth that smelled like disinfectant. An eye-catching waitress dressed in blue went back and forth from the kitchen. I photographed her from behind, her glossy hair and little ass. Xu gave me a judgmental look and I deleted the picture. She didn't speak to me the whole way to the metro. When I asked her, like a six-year-old girl, if she still loved me, she laughed faintly. "Go home," she said through her teeth, not looking me in the face. That night I slept badly and dreamt Xu's thighs were fish, wet and scaly, and I caressed them tenderly and fearfully. I woke up at eight with a fever. No—it wasn't a fever, the thermometer read 36. I was sick in a subtler, less recognizable sense. On the paper, a picture of an underwater cathedral, in Qiandao Lake, the one with the deformed fish. It was a burial site from a distant era.

22

Chest

I slept little. I didn't watch TV because I couldn't concentrate. I woke up in the night with a taste in my mouth that reminded me of rusty abandoned cars. Monday morning, in class, I found an insect shell on my sweater. It was smooth and pearlescent. I nudged it delicately, but it didn't want to detach from my chest. At home that evening I saw a nasty mosquito on the shower door. I squished it and it spurted more blood than I thought possible. Then that night as I was nodding off, I felt a little spider on my lips, followed by a soft, vaporous sensation: a spiderweb. The insects increased as the days went on. Some were really there, others figments of imagination. I dreamt. Some crawled out from doorjambs, others through the fissure separating dream from reality. That fissure kept widening, like an untreated wound. Night-black roaches scurried into the room and then vanished under the furniture. Surreptitious gnats, evanescent as dust particles, followed me to the metro, orbiting my head. Red ants followed me to the market. Insects of all kinds. They emerged from the dark into the harsh light of my room, panicky with hunger.

The exterminator came and I waited for him in the hallway, staring at the green emergency exit signs. For days I had been wondering what those insects might mean. Nothing, of course. They weren't the ones I dreamt the first three months after Ruben's death, every night, as I came off my grief like a bender. They were just bugs. They existed for themselves, for nature, and not to convey some message to me. But my overwhelmed mind had become a vacuum that sucked up every symbol, every insignificant bit of my life. Suddenly, sitting uncomfortably on the gray carpet, I realized that a line in my relationship with Xu had been crossed. I didn't know exactly what that line was. Between my body and hers. Between self-preservation and total surrender. Now that the line had been crossed, anything could be done. To me. To my body. An inexorable force, stronger than my mind, compelled me to obey. Because of that new, titillating weakness, that afternoon I let her lead me to the slaughterhouse without a word.

Hailun Road station was big and uneven. An old man gazing dully into space. Xu was dressed like a bored but fabulous hooker out of a nineties Japanese movie. An expensive Coke-color kimono over daisy dukes. I'm trying to remember everything, every point on the crooked timeline of my love for Xu, the logical points and the symbolic points, like the Christian timeline based on lots of promises and a big cross stuck in the ground. We stopped in an alley that smelled like rotting meat, and went through the service door of an abandoned mall. It was enormous. There were faded signs proclaiming vitality. ENJOY LIFE. I WILL GIVE YOU ALL MY LOVE. ALWAYS BE HAPPY. Xu was going to meet someone. Waiting against the wall, she ate pink and white swirl candy. A little girl arrived. Or rather, a woman who looked like a little girl. She had a round, puffy face, hair in greasy braids, and a dress the color of cotton candy. She handed Xu a sparkly sachet and left. Xu opened it and pulled out the yellow pills. She said: "No more fear, I promise, open your mouth," her hoarse words making a monstrous echo. I stuck out my tongue, saw it reflected in the mirrored wall: it was gray and furry as if I had licked cement. It scared me. I was sure it was the pollution, but my first thought was: *It's the things I said. All the expressions of love I never should have uttered.*

I followed Xu to the exit. I felt the pill fizzing and dissolving in my mouth like an Alka-Seltzer. I thought of the thousand fevers I'd had when I was little, Ruben and I, our little heads boiling together on the pillow, our sweaty, dreamless sleep. We walked along the river. On the opposite shore, a row of vacant buildings. There was a quiet that buzzed with old motor scooters in the distance, and cold laughter muffled by the wind. We passed a row of produce stands selling muddy bulbs and little brown apples. Then fabric sellers. Dusty bolts of cloth on the sidewalk. A stand selling socks with the ideogram for fortune embroidered upside-down on the ankles. A bride sitting outside a house on a red chair, waiting for something, her eyes blank, her rumpled veil grazing the asphalt.

23

Skin

We arrived as the sun started to set. The slaughterhouse was massive. A slate-gray monolith of steel and concrete, broken up by obsessive, robust columns, and grates that, jaw-like, gripped the walls all the way up to the eaves. Tall zigzag staircases wound upward between the enclosure walls, which were twenty inches thick and hollow for temperature regulation: the lambs' bodies, as they moved upward, had to lose heat, had to reach the proper chill for slaughter. Xu had explained all this on the metro, careful to note that she did not want to be interrupted. She spoke slowly, laying out the historical and aesthetic details of that hellish place, as the train filled with more and more people at each stop, their bodies pressed together, with expressionless faces and trendy clothes. Custom designed in the 1920s for a schizoid city, fragmented into international concessions, the new slaughterhouse was created to supply top-quality meat to all the foreign communities. The butchery had to be done in accordance with the highest Western standards of efficiency and in a setting of impeccable European elegance. Cutting-edge techniques, the new concept of hygiene, no expense spared, in a winding modernist labyrinth inside sophisticated art deco building. Occidental grace on the outside, a psychosis of abstractions and concrete on the inside. Four floors surrounding a sun-filled center: the platform onto which the bodies dropped.

"Are you feeling it?" she asked, as we crossed the intersecting bridges. It was a maze that led nowhere. You entered a dark room and then emerged into a patchwork of concrete passageways, which met and then parted. Outside the latticework, a desolate panorama of seventies high-rises and tower blocks, and a murky light.

"I don't know. How am I supposed to feel?"

"I told you. You stop being afraid."

"But I'm not . . ."

"Impossible. Everyone is always afraid. It's fear that pushes us to keep living, get out of bed in the morning.

Fear of death, of time passing, of making the wrong choices . . ."

"That's not true. Not everything is motivated by fear."

"But it is. Even we're together because of fear."

"Of what?"

"Solitude, for one."

"No. I'm with you because of love."

"Love is fear, too, if you look at it close enough."

"What do you mean? Fear of what?"

"Of what you think, of what I think, of how long I can leave you on your own. You love me because you're afraid of how my actions affect you."

"That doesn't make sense."

"But it does. Don't be naive. Love is born of absence. Inconstancy. The seed of fear grows in the intervals where the other is gone. Fear that they won't come back. And that fear blossoms into love."

For a moment I considered it. I followed her reasoning in my head as we crossed the bridges, going in and out of the big dark rooms. I followed her reasoning and I realized it was risky to follow. Follow it all the way through.

"You're a cynic. Love is more than that."

"Hear your voice? You sound calm. It's hitting you."

We were inside. On one of the ramps.

"You're even hotter when you're not shaking like a baby bird. Lie down and close your eyes."

I lay back on the cold, rough ground.

"Tell me something else."

"About love?"

"No. About this place."

She moved closer to my ear. She sighed. Then, caressing me, she told me the whole story. After the slaughterhouse closed down, it became a processing plant and then a pharmaceutical company, then was abandoned in 2002. After that, the Shanghai International College of Design and Innovation decided to restore it and make it into a cultural hub. It didn't work. It was a grim, uninviting space that inspired desolate thoughts in anyone who entered. Sun came through the glass in the ceiling and lit the floor like something mechanical, a device. Through that shadow and light, the narrow ramps propelled you, like a lab rat, toward the exterior, and then turned you back to the internal maze.

Over time, cafés appeared, closed down. Boutiques with outrageous clothing. Closed down. Now the section where the carcasses had been kept was a gourmet restaurant no one went to. The waitresses wore glittering red dresses that sparkled in the daylight like the plumage of strange birds. The first floor housed a club for Ferrari owners. It was strange to think of them there, talking about cars and speed, life's externalities. In there, in that abattoir, it was all interior. If you closed your eyes, you could see the lambs' pain combined with the centuries-old hunger of the Chinese, and the mind-bending philosophy, torturous gardens, slender empresses with bound feet. Out in the city, nothing can be imagined, because everything is already there, and trying leads to an excess of images that makes everything hurt.

I looked around. The leaden sheen of concrete between grates and dying plants. Ramps like vertebrae and compressed tendons. The place didn't suggest anything beautiful, anything healthy. Some buildings don't survive history to communicate anything—they survive by mistake, by the blind endurance of matter. I looked up at the ceiling. At the enormous, west-facing windows. Xu told me there were two reasons for them. One was spiritual, the other physical. According to Buddhism, facing west would help the lambs reincarnate, and because the wind in this chaotic, turbulent city blows west, dissipating the smell of slaughter. I saw Xu's cold eyes focused on my body, saw her scrutinizing my skin, and thought, she was right: I was less afraid and I did love her less. And it was a relief. It was wonderful.

It lasted a half hour. Her neat, oyster-white teeth, dotted with saliva, traced commas across my wrist and, for a moment, stopped its beat, my thoughts. She said "I like you so much," she kept repeating it, like a dumb poem you have to memorize in second grade. *I like you so much. I like you so much. I like you so much.* Words of affection are sometimes nothing more than incantations. Forms of control. Like a snake charmer with a snake. She bit harder. Higher, along the shoulder. A groan came out of me like a lever being pushed on a machine. A clutch to a rarely used gear. With my eyes clenched shut, as I felt her tongue move downward, I imagined the lambs in their little cages, and I started to cry, and I couldn't stop, I couldn't stop crying and imagining.

"Stop whimpering. Don't you love me?"

"I do . . . I love you so much."

"Then stop it. Only babies cry like that."

Seen like this, seen from the slaughterhouse floor, seen in that oppressive light, my skin looked different. It seemed like an inanimate thing. Like the lambskin of shoes or a purse. Something you wear. Something that had once been alive and needy and now is just an accessory. Medical attention to skin only began in the sixteenth century. Previously, it was considered an inert sac holding our insides. Then they realized it was something else. That it breathed. That it had a life apart from what it protected. That it was not a sac at all. It was an organ like any other, only more still. Patient. A martyr immolated on the pyre of bones, exposed to everything, ready for anything. To meet the world, this filthy, disastrous world, and try not to let it in.

24

Legs

Back home that night, there was a sheet of paper on my door. It warned me that a typhoon was coming. PLEASE CLOSE ALL DOORS AND WINDOWS AND LIMIT OUTDOOR ACTIVITY. The notice was from six hours earlier, so the apocalypse was imminent. I locked myself inside, in the dark, until it began. I heard shattering glass and an ominous roaring wind. Erratic, sideways rain skidded over everything, riding the gray air. Empty windows. Asphyxiating high-rises cutting into the sky. Sky shriveled like dead matter. No light, only a shaky blur. Teeming human masses. Dark heads and umbrellas taut like a second skin. Bruise-colored asphalt. A propulsion of legs and fluttering raincoats. The gold of the temple glittering with death. Xu sent me a text but the vibration of the phone was lost in the tremor of everything else. By the time I saw it there were six more. *When I write to you you have to answer immediately, that's how this works. Now there are going to be consequences.*

I mouthed the word *consequences*. It sounded like the wind when it blows against something fixed: walls, buildings. Language can be as aggressive and senseless as a typhoon. It depends on who uses it. It depends on the destructive charge of their not loving you enough. I slid under the covers. It was probably three A.M. and my head was spinning. Still with my eyes closed I could sense the bluish rays of city light like messages from boundless skies.

After that I spent a few days away from myself. Myself was a place I no longer wanted to be. Xu kept her distance too. She didn't call. By now I was used to the push and pull. Unfortunately those intervals of silence didn't diminish my feelings for her. On the contrary, love crept into every gap in communication, like the roots of a monstrous vine.

I thought about the lambs constantly. The ones from the slaughterhouse and the ones all over the world. I thought about them with affection and guilt. I learned that in China in 1500 BC, masses of them were sacrificed to the god Shang Di because they symbolized eternal beauty and truth. They say that the Tang emperor, during a period of extreme drought, turned into a lamb himself, even though it meant his own sacrifice. His blood traced humble words on the arid earth. A kind of poem. That night, all over China, a violent rain fell.

I stopped eating. I stopped going to class. I watched Asian TV shows all night. One was called *1 Liter of Tears* and it was a true story about a girl with a degenerative disorder. Inexorably, episode by episode, that shy, beautiful girl lost the use of her legs, and eventually everything else, but her only regret was becoming a burden to her loved ones. When her father and mother fed her, she cried with shame.

One of those days, sometime between afternoon and evening, Xu posted a selfie with Kelly on WeChat. They were smiling. They had happy eyes and disheveled hair. They were in Xu's room. It was impossible to tell if they'd been kissing, if Xu had left a little bite mark on her neck, if they had just resurfaced from intimate, profound conversation like dolphins.

Sometimes I went out. I walked until I felt weak. The international quarter took on a sinister aspect, with its hydrated trees and immaculate marble stairs, as if the entire space were a mise-en-scène to fool people, induce an irrational serenity. Occasionally strangers would talk to me on the street, maybe to ask for directions, or to take my picture because I'm blonde and Western, but on my end, the sentences came out partial and incomprehensible, like language had shattered and everyone had a shard of glass in their mouths, a fragment of sense, a blind vibration of vocal cords. Sometimes I spoke, too, to strangers, in a language that was no longer Chinese but hadn't yet reverted to Italian. It happened at the ticket booth in the metro whenever I tried to buy a ticket, or at the supermarket when I asked for pumpkin baozi. I stammered exhaustedly, reaching for words that didn't come; I was stuck in an empty space, a lingua franca of the unconscious made of tears and silence. I burst out crying under the harsh fluorescent light of the convenience store, putting together a phrase that seemed like a desperate prayer, a senseless prayer no one understood.

I slept all day long. The school called incessantly and the ringing telephone invaded my dreams, transforming into the dismal siren of Day-Glo ambulances speeding down the endless roads of a city that looked like Shanghai, except Xu wasn't there. Sometimes I dreamt of the lambs. Small and terrified in their pens, immobilized and juicy on lavish Easter tables, caricatured on Easter cards.

On February 1, my dismissal letter came. I looked up at the colorless, snow-laden sky and thought of Ruben, his blue eyes disappearing behind his eyelids as they closed for the last time, and somehow I knew that he hadn't struggled. That he had let go. I knew that I was letting myself go because he had let himself go, because that's how we are, we let ourselves go.

25

Muscles

Xu showed up again on February 2. With the usual telegraphic WeChat message: *Jingan metro, 5 P.M.* I read the message three times, curled up in bed. It was six in the morning. WeChat had the bare-bones design of eighties technology, bland and a bit sad, which I had come to associate with her understated communiqués. There weren't even prepopulated stickers to pad conversations. You had to download them from an external site. She had a ton: cats in glasses, smirking bats. Where did they come from? From another chat, from another feeling? Sometimes, when I asked her a basic question about our relationship, the kind suffused with need and fear, like, *Do you think about me?* Xu would flood our chat with those garish silly faces, frenetic meaningless animals.

A language that flattened, belittled, invalidated my talk of love.

On my way there I kept one eye on the phone, waiting for something more. A kiss, a happy emoji. But no. Nothing. She knew a few words were enough to pull me in. The conversation could remain minimal, like traffic lights, because my obedience was immediate, responsive, as to a road sign, a command to stop or slow down. I went down to the metro, wove through the bustling crowd. I dropped my purple metro card, recovered it under a seat in a sea of old gum. I knew that this time, too, would last only the blink of an eye. Every time Xu came back it was for only a little while: a prelude to vanishing. A wrong word, a crying fit, a confrontation, any discrepancy with the role she had assigned me would make her disappear again. She was an impassive swift and I wasn't her nest; I was a twig to perch on for a moment's pause.

We went back to the slaughterhouse. In the days of Xu's absence, I looked up everything about it, I was obsessed. I hated it, but I was obsessed. I read every article on it I could find, lying in bed eating lollipops and White Rabbits. I learned that when it was first built, it was one of the biggest slaughterhouses in the world, and now it was the only one left with that type of architecture, that horrific precision and surrealist streak. I learned that the floor was designed to be rough to keep the lambs from slipping on their own blood. And that in the 1930s, twelve hundred lambs died there every day, after a grueling trip up dark, endless ramps, and being penned at each level before heading up the next one. The pigs, too slow to climb, remained on the ground floor: death came to them in one fell swoop.

"Your complexion is terrible," said Xu at the doorway, kissing me tepidly.

"I missed you."

"I missed you, too, of course."

"Then why . . ."

"Why what?"

"Forget it."

The lambs were branded on narrow bridges and then killed once they reached the top, where gravity drained their blood, causing the scraps to fall and reducing the weight of the carcass. Extermination at the Shanghai abattoir unfolded in several short, meticulously realized scenes: it was an obscene theater of death, impervious to the slightest blunder or snag. The cold, perfect function-ality of the Chinese slaughterhouse, its mechanized production and hyperrational stamp, had inspired the design of the first automotive assembly lines. The idea of a complex product created out of many small parts, like a mind dissected to infinity. Slaughter as psychoanalysis.

We went all the way to the top floor. We didn't have to take the stairs; there was a glass elevator, installed in the days when they tried to turn that morbid site into a shopping center. There wasn't really any difference, I said to myself. The kind with stores was only a more abstract form of consumption: you didn't see the blood; you didn't see the underweight children bent over sewing machines. Xu pressed 5. The elevator bolted up too fast, the air rushed out of my chest. Five was deserted. The floor was an enormous glass sunburst, segmented like a beehive. This was the dying place. I looked down. You could see everything below, like we were up in a terrible sky. The twisted steel, the bridges, the slanted light from the slats. People appearing and disappearing behind concrete spirals like hallucinations. I lay back and closed my eyes as Xu kissed me. Naked on the glass, we were bathed in a pathological, unseasonable sunlight rising from underneath like embers. As Xu's mouth traversed my body, I felt grateful that I saw only blackness and not the small, stunned deaths of the lambs. I felt grateful for all the things I didn't see. That I didn't see the clammy bodies of crammed-in calves climbing the ramp, lowing. That I didn't hear the sharp, piercing cries, signs of fear or life.

That, even if Xu didn't love me, at least with every passing day my brother's face grew hazier in my mind, like a sky upswept by clouds.

Then it happened. She bit me so hard, on my neck. She hurt me. I shivered, my back arched. I couldn't speak, object. I thought a human body shouldn't be this frightened. I remembered a deer I saw on a country road one night three years before. It suddenly appeared in front of our car on our way back from Lake Bracciano. Ruben was the first to shout, seeing the shape in the headlights, the yellow eyes and the outline of the torso. My father braked; the deer dodged the car with an agile leap. In the halo of the lights I'd seen everything: the tremor, the muscular reaction to danger. Only animal bodies are made to fill up with fright. Not human ones. Only animals can be that afraid, because nothing in the world ever dissuades them from wanting to stay alive. I felt Xu's small, bony hand between my legs. A cry gurgled out from my mouth.

26

Hair

We like love because it's an edible feeling. After it has been transferred from the brain to the skin, the genitals, it can be licked and sucked. It can linger on the tongue like a foolproof pill. Hate is edible too. Both, after being digested and expelled by the organism, can leave horrid traces of desire. Sly, slow, indigestible toxins. You can't always recover.

We went to the slaughterhouse every day.

The strangeness became routine.

The yellow pill, the winding ramps, the echoes of concrete and glass. Before biting into me she'd given me exaggerated compliments about my skin being like hers. White, instantly red in the sun. Pale, veiny nipples like broken clocks. We were dolls made from the same silicone mold, with such different minds that only our bodies could communicate. Communicate endlessly, through the flesh, in search of something we could never find.

Everything was fair game. Loose skin, scabs, epidermis, fat. A little nest of dirty blonde hair, greasy with shampoo, that I'd collected from the shower drain and placed on her tongue once we reached the narrow ramps of the butchery. They weren't offerings, they didn't symbolize anything, they didn't bring us any closer to love. Xu would lower her eyes and accept everything, the way I had accepted thinking of nothing else but her, day and night.

She kissed my eyelids and nose; she licked my hair like a cat. She put one hand between my legs and with the other drew hearts on my cheeks, with her fingertip, then with her pointy nail. In ancient China, before a wedding, the bride's hair had to be brushed by a happy person. A happy, fortunate mother of many children. No exceptions allowed. Then there was the crying ritual. This was when the bride saw her parents for the last time. Afterward they cut a lock of her hair and of the groom's and tied them together, inseparably. Their entwined hair was kept in a safe place and never disentangled. The powder and fermented rice, the milky water with which it was washed, made it shine for years. Hair makes the best relic, because it doesn't decay. It outlasts love and death, the deaths of those whose heads it graced. That's why it's the preferred bodily totem in witchcraft. My hair, I conserved it all for Xu, like flowers in a meadow waiting to be gathered.

Sometimes Xu would choose the thin skin that spanned from my clavicle to my head. My head. That, she would never eat. Not even a lick on the skin. Not out of respect, but terror of the sadness inside. My sadness was like hers: dangerous. Our sadness was the most dangerous thing that had ever happened to us. It made our feelings loud and unreliable, like trains about to derail. When I looked at myself in the mirror at night, in my bright, blue-lit bathroom on the thirty-first floor of the Starlight Hotel, and I examined my fresh wounds, my red patches, the tooth marks on my thighs, I felt a little sorry for myself, or a lot sorry, which is the closest I managed to come to self-love.

That Saturday it snowed. The flowerbeds around the hotel filled up with snow. The tips of the grass poked out like stubble. I stopped to look at them, pensive. I wondered what Ruben thought. Of that relationship, of Xu, of what I'd become. Naturally, Ruben could no longer think anything, but I wondered all the same. Like a hopeless ritual. Like a prayer. His thoughts, which were just the underside of mine—a pavement of the unconscious and fear, hope too perhaps—followed me in my dreams and gave me no rest.

During the night I woke up with a start. The fire alarm was blaring. I rushed out the door, barefoot and dazed, but it was a false alarm. The boy with the green hair and tired face came, crouched down on the carpet, and pressed a button under the security exit sign across from my door. The silence resumed. As the boy disappeared down the hall, I had an urge to stop him. To shout: *Come back, let's talk for a minute. Please don't leave me all alone with my love for Xu.*

27

Scab

I stopped hoping for her to love me back. The hope died along with winter's final throes. It was only February 20, but a pale sun had begun to brighten the streets at midday, illuminating the puddles from the previous night. I started following Xu on the days she was away from me. Dressed in black, eco-leather shorts, fishnets, down in the metro among the whirring trains and the strangers, and I discovered that she had changed schools. Now she was taking a class at Fudan University, near her place. I tailed her at a distance, like a virus waiting to latch on. Eyes shining with fear, my black hoodie hugging my face, I followed her to the campus. The buildings at Fudan were imitations of Western buildings that no longer existed. Greek columns, high renaissance, two-bit baroque. Xu stood there for a moment, at the entrance, while the facial recognition scanner made sure that Xu was Xu, Xu and no one else, and I got a knot in my stomach because that irreproducible genetic composition named Xu was the only one I wanted, the only one that was going to destroy me.

It's strange when the hope that one's love will be reciprocated dies. It's strange because it's a fantasy that falls apart even before you know you had it: the fantasy of coupledom, of being essential to another person. It falls apart before you knew it was there. It all happens so fast that only the body is able to keep up. Time becomes physical, muscular. Blood is quicker than the brain. Abrasions on the arms and chest, on the fingers, form scabs. The skin defends itself, regenerates, and in regenerating, forgets it was ever wounded.

Hope dies and everything slows back down. The heart beats, fatigued, stifled by the bones. Old thoughts resurface, depleted. The antidepressants I took to boost my mood and ability to tolerate reality, my vital instinct, slid down my throat compliantly but no longer sufficed.

Once in a while it was hard to find a quiet spot at the slaughterhouse. There were photogenic girls everywhere, with teddy bears and miniskirts, painted faces. They all wanted to be photographed in the art deco palace where the lambs perished. A dreamy Instagram-ready stage set. A "cool" place. They smiled against the light, against the background of the twisting ramps, instilling that unhealthy place with a false vitality. Sometimes Xu and I couldn't find room for our mini-massacre, our love massacre, and we went around a thousand times, until at least the top floor, the glass floor, the coldest part, cleared out. We lay down and started all over again.

I undressed mechanically, in Xu's predetermined order, which was as precise as the order in which logograms are to be traced. From top to bottom, left to right. Never the shoes before the shirt, never the right sleeve first. I doubted there was any logic to that rule. I doubted there was much logic to most of Xu's decisions. The only thing that counted was reducing my will, my free will, to the minimum. And that light on the ceiling . . . that light dazed me. It wasn't natural. It was designed to avoid mistakes: to aggrandize the details of the slaughter. Like a diagnostic light pointed at you. Right where it hurts. The red inside of a mouth, the burst capillaries of an eye. I squeezed mine shut and let myself be fucked.

As she fucked me, I closed my eyes and breathed. I imagined my childhood, or a generic one, clusters of boisterous children on a lawn in the sun, a picnic, a loving mother, days passed in blankets and reassurances. Sometimes we came at the same time, Xu and I, an orgasm like a typhoon that bends trees and takes your breath away, but really they were two different orgasms, because I was wounded and she wasn't. Little bubbles of blood studded my skin. Sometimes I touched them, quiet and wistful, the way you'd stroke a flower that the sun hadn't opened. It was night, once again.

The last day of February. As it rained outside, and we were kissing on the twisting stairwell, I saw something in the darkness. A shadow. I jerked back and sat down. It was him. Ruben. Lying over a step, sick, still alive. It was just a shadow but it was clearly him. I didn't have the courage to approach. I didn't have the strength to shout. Maybe I'd taken too many yellow pills; maybe I was just too tired. Maybe the pill interfered with antidepressants? Mesmerized, sitting half-naked on the cement stair, I tried to understand why my brother had come. I really tried, but sleep took over, a torrid, surreal sleep.

That evening on my way home, I noticed the first flowers at the sidewalk's edge. At that instant I felt my phone vibrate: an email from my parents. I thought it was one of the usual ones, full of unbearable affection, which I never replied to, or replied just with pictures of the city, perfunctory blurry photos off my phone. But it was something else. They said that they had found, in a backpack of my brother's, a letter for me. It was scanned and attached. My heart flipped. I rushed home, drank a little plum wine and gathered up my strength. I opened it.

28

Scars

Over the course of two months, my body had drifted gracelessly away from Ruben's, so thin, eaten away by pain, still alive. Sluggish, pale, like an old dress. It was March and the dust on the windows sparkled in the sun. My mother, after coming back from the clinic, was planting difficult flowers in the dry soil of our little garden. I was already looking for a job in China and eating little cookies full of artificial flavoring. I looked out from the balcony, imagining things that weren't there that now I don't remember.

At the funeral, on May 2, at the Gothic church far from our house, my parents noticed the additional ten pounds in my ruched black cotton dress, you could tell by their expression. But fortunately they were occupied with more significant emotions. I wish I had a clearer memory of the eulogy, the sermon, the carving on the wooden casket, the deafening swallows out the windows, things like that. But it's all background. Brain pavement. Flashes of black clothes, eyes, my arms folded over my stomach, over my extra ten pounds.

Michele had arrived at the funeral early in a gray suit and hugged all my relatives, as if he had anything to do with their pain. This bothered me so much that I sat three rows away. Now and then, as the priest listlessly recited the ritual phrases, I turned to look at his fresh boyish face. It's something people say: *fresh-faced.* As if people were comparable to dairy products. To edible products stolen from animal flesh. Michele had small hands and thin hair. Before we met, we had talked online for a month. He had seventy-three followers and all he posted were clips from new wave movies. In his profile picture, snapped hastily in some square in Spain, his smile projected a melancholy left unexplored out of laziness.

It was Sunday. I think it was Sunday, when Ruben was buried. As they lowered the casket into the ground, and we watched, it was five in the afternoon, and Michele squeezed my cold hand in his, and I had dry eyes, and the thing in my mind was not yet pain but stupor, at the instant it touched the bottom, the wind was gentle and dusty with earth against our cold, coat-clad bodies, and it felt like Sunday, the epitome of Sunday; like those long childhood Sundays when I was waiting for something but didn't know what, and the adults tried to fill the time, and I didn't yet know that time had to be filled, that it was dangerous to leave it empty.

In China, as February was ending and spring was slowly starting, I had hit bottom, but the bottom kept dropping further. It was like endless digging, down and down and down, while Xu appeared and disappeared, appeared and disappeared, like a dizzying hallucination, like a dying light bulb, until digging through that bottomless darkness, the darkness in my head, I disappeared too.

Sometimes when I closed my eyes at night, I saw Shanghai. I pictured it the way it really was: massive and frenetic, opulent and poor, boundless. But in my imagination, at a certain point, the showy skyscrapers and crumbling warehouses became Roman ruins and potholes and my brother's spotless clinic. As if space weren't a matter of being in it, being in one place and not another, but an ungraspable idea that could be molded by suffering or slip through the fingers like sand. When I shook myself out of that confused half-sleep, I reached, in the dark, for Ruben's picture. Not the phone. Not the turmoil of Xu's texts. I just wanted a little peace. I turned on the light, got up, and looked outside. The street under the streetlights. Even the street is just an idea: the impulse to go somewhere, away from those who have hurt you, or closer to those who love you.

It was March 2, six P.M. My mental collapse had already gone through one full cycle, chronologically and corporeally, and had left me drained and with several small scars that may or may not fade. Some would for sure. Others, with their grainy little bumps, would forever remind me of what I was capable of doing to myself. Another school emailed me with a job opportunity. I wrote an enthusiastic reply, but lingered on the "send" button for an hour, undecided whether to click. At some point, I heard my phone buzz on the bed. It vibrated, muffled, once and then twice, and then again, under a mountain of covers, under a mountain of feelings. A totally dull sound. No melody, no pretense of beauty. The white noise of my waiting, of the frail, stunted desire to be loved. I shoved it in my pocket and went out for a walk.

I walked for hours. All the way to Zhongshan Park. There were people dancing everywhere, as if possessed by a physical, animal joy. They danced and thrashed about. They laughed. They wore red and yellow and blue. And old people playing mahjong, hunched over game boards. People singing Peking opera. Septuagenarians doing the waltz. I felt overwhelmed by all that overbearing, performative joy, the frenzy to externalize happiness. I didn't understand it entirely but it was intoxicating. It was a memory I wanted to keep forever.

I ate at an empty restaurant on the eleventh floor of a shopping center on Nanjing Road. Out the window I could see the Molly statue from behind, her twenty-foot tall body, her black ponytails. A very pale, very pretty waitress came. I didn't feel like speaking Chinese, so I pointed to a glossy picture on the menu: a plate of vegetable ramen, gleaming red, full of vitality. I smiled, gesturing as if I understood nothing of the language. I was foreign: foreign to China, foreign to myself. I felt a strange peace: the kind unleashed when you hit bottom, because the mind is free from the strain of trying not to fall.

I chewed slowly, unhungrily, watching children unwrapping chocolates and couples kissing shyly. I was tempted to think of Ruben, but I focused on the taste of the acrid sauce over the thin noodles, the sensation they left on my tongue. I thought about the past-present-future: in Chinese grammar, it's all one thing. A twisted plant of which we see only the flower. We admire it, that beautiful flower, and believe in it, because we don't know how gnarled, fragile, monstrous the roots are. I thought of the plant in the window of my room in Rome. I picked up the phone and called home for the first time.

"Mama, can you hear me?"

"Darling. It's you. Is everything all right? It's so nice to hear from you."

"Yeah. What happened to the plant in my window? Have you watered it? Is it still alive?"

"Huh? What plant? I don't know. Is that why you called?"

"Go look."

"I'm in bed, but I don't remember any plant in your room."

"Then it's dead. When it died did you keep it? At least press one of the leaves in a book?"

"Stop it. What is this all about?"

"Nothing. Ruben gave it to me. For our birthday. You should remember."

On the other end of the line there was a long silence. When you know a person well, their silence is braille; you can perceive the contours of everything left unsaid. Listening to that silence, on that intercontinental call, gave me a flash read of my mother's feelings, how she had handled her grief after I left. At that moment I realized this was why I never called my parents or answered their calls. I didn't have the strength to bear their braille, the bumps and hollows of their pain. I already had my own.

"I'm sorry. That's not why I called. I didn't call about the letter either. Let's talk about something else. Is Dad okay?"

"Yes. We miss you. How's Shanghai?"

"Mom. Places are what you make of them. It depends on you."

"What do you mean?"

"Nothing. Shanghai is incredible. Everything is beautiful, everything is impressive. The food is weird and wonderful. It has character. Like it could attack you. Make you sad, or really happy. Listen, Mom, I want to tell you about someone I met."

"Of course. Tell me everything."

I stayed on the phone for an hour, until my credit ran out. I talked to my father. I called my two closest friends, Emma and Olga: I hadn't answered their messages in ages.

I told everyone the whole story. Going on and on like an overflowing river

"What did you say her name was? Shu?"

"Xu. It's pronounced Xu."

I repeated her name with religious insistence, as if even then, in conversation with another person, I was calling, summoning, trying to catch her. My throat was dry; my heart was dry. I felt like a dry creek on a desolate mountain. And I didn't want advice, from any of them. I wanted banal reassurances, clichés, the empty and optimistic phrases you say to people you love so they can sleep better at night. And that's exactly what I got. A slew of variations on *Whatever is meant to happen will happen* and *Don't worry*. It was a liberation. From my mother, my father, from my friends. I turned off my phone and the park felt different. The couples had disbanded, people wandered alone with little nervous dogs. There was a tepid, inconstant sun, continually chased by a swarm of clouds. The landscape, life, suddenly seemed to clash less with my state of mind. I got up. I decided I had to do something. I owed it to my brother. His letter, on graph paper, had said: *Wherever you go, I'll be inside you. Like a second skin, but deeper down. Recognize me, keep on loving me. Loving yourself. I will never leave you.*

29

Severed Arms

For Xu's birthday, March 6, we went to Donglin Temple, in a Shanghai suburb. A temple built in 1308 and repeatedly destroyed by war and fire. Inside there was an eight-story statue of the bodhisattva Guanyin sitting on a six-foot lotus. She had several arms and a stern, striking face. She was the goddess of mercy. "Have mercy on me," I said to her aloud, and my voice seemed to come from somewhere dusty, like the dirty broom closet in a house.

Legend has it that Guanyin was a girl who wanted to become a Buddhist nun. Her father was against it; he wanted to marry her off to a prosperous match like his other daughters. So he banished her. Years later he fell ill, and a monk told him, "In order to recover you must drink a potion distilled from the arms and eyes of a person who willingly gives them to you." On the peak of Fragrant Mountain there was a bodhisattva of mercy, the monk added. So the king sent a messenger, who upon arrival at the mountain discovered that the bodhisattva was the man's daughter. The girl, her skin pale and clammy, her body malnourished, her mind perhaps in a fog of hunger, cut off her arms and gouged out her eyes and sent them over. The father drank those parts of his daughter's body and his illness vanished. His daughter went to find him to explain what she had done, to make him cry. A form of sacrifice, a form of love. The two get confused when one has been loved too little.

That night, at the slaughterhouse, after coming down from an orgasm and an aimless conversation under the influence of the yellow pill, I looked at my hands: four, six, eight, of them, like Guanyin. Clearly I'd dosed wrong, and too many yellow pills push you out of yourself like too much broth spilling out of a bowl. I looked around. The slaughterhouse shone. A vast, gloomy mirror of glass and steel reflecting nothing. I vaguely remembered that, when Xu had gone to find a bathroom, I had opened the little foil ball she kept in her purse and taken another pill. For no reason. No reason besides taking everything down to the last drop.

I tried to stand, but the weight from all those arms made me stumble. Some were soft, unmanageable, others had tensed muscles and were carrying things in their hands. Weapons, torture devices. I'd seen the statue holding these instruments. But I never understood what they had to do with mercy. My head felt like an old pot, hanging empty and dinged from overuse. I moved sluggishly. The light from the hole in the ceiling blazed straw yellow. Spring making its way in. Slowly, with dull persistence, erasing winter. My heart was beating too fast, somewhere between the tangle of arms, some of which were folded across my chest, a mirage of resignation. I squinted—too much light. It beamed down from the top of the empty hall, through the hole created in the structure's center to ensure constant sunlight—a constant view of the massacre. I couldn't bear it. I couldn't face the coming of another season. The flowers blossoming on the outskirts of cities, fragrant with rebirth, the sky opening like the skin's pores in a steam bath, spring turning to summer as if everything could regenerate. I trembled; my vision blurred. I thought I was going to faint.

Xu appeared. Back from the bathroom, yellow in the light, a dazzling executioner. I felt the truth falling from my mouth like vomit.

"Tell me. Why do you always disappear like that?"

"You sound weird. How many pills did you take?"

"Answer me."

"You know why. I need to think."

"You can't think with me around?"

"Of course not. Thought requires space."

"I can think even while I'm in your arms. That's enough space for me."

"We're different. You know that. You love me precisely because I go away."

"Don't try to psychoanalyze me. You don't know anything about me."

"Actually, I do. You're as easy to read as a children's book. You love me because one moment I'm there, the next I'm not. Like your brother."

"Excuse me?"

"Admit it. When he was alive you were jealous of him. You wanted the affection he got, the attention that went to him, his light . . . That wasn't love. It was a morbid attachment that fed on your frustration at not being like him. Your failed attempts to emulate him. Now that he's dead, finally you can love him for real. Because now you have more than him."

"You're a monster . . . You . . ."

"I'm a monster, sure. I'm a monster because I'm free, because I sleep with whoever I want, because I don't want to answer to anyone?"

"No. You're a monster because you take advantage of my fragility, because you take my pain and use it against me."

"Think you're so good at figuring out everyone else? Seems to me like you were always a willing participant . . . You were out to hurt yourself. You wanted to punish yourself. Punish yourself for outliving your brother, his death, your jealousy . . . Punish yourself because you always wanted to take his place, and your wish came true . . ."

I was shaking violently, but fortunately the pill's calming effect kept my mind from producing searing panic. Xu placed a hand on my cheek, as if for a caress, but then didn't move, like she just wanted to check whether I still existed.

"Don't touch me!"

"Oh, stop crying. You're ugly when you cry . . ."

I wiped away my tears with an angry gesture.

"Go away! I want you out of my life! My sacrifice is over."

"Sacrifice?"

"I don't want to see you anymore. Ever again."

She fell to her knees. On the dusty, dirty floor. An unexpected act. Like a marionette whose strings were suddenly cut. "Don't leave me, please," she said, and she started to cry. I felt an urge to come closer, to put my hand in her hair and rub her head, like Guanyin would have done. Like I would have up until a few hours ago. But something rigid, unmovable, had taken over me. I wanted my eyes and arms back, the flesh I had offered in exchange for the mirage of affection. My mind was confused, assailed by flashing images: the glittering skyscrapers, the noisy creatures at the insect market, and the old fable where all the forest animals bring Buddha presents, but the rabbit has nothing, and so offers the gift of his own life.

I stared at Xu without moving a muscle, without saying a word. There was nothing in her eyes, only need, and her tears turned to weeping, louder and more shrill, becoming an endlessly echoing *don't leave me, please*: a broken cheesy music box, an untimely plea directed at the figures from her childhood, not me. That's not how I'd imagined her crying. So volatile, so irreparable.

"Do you know what I used to eat when I was little?" she said.

"No, what?"

"Dog. And other stuff for boys. Did you know our food is divided into boy food and girl food? They . . . they wanted me to be a boy . . ."

"You told me."

She looked up at me, her eyes wet. Her expression was different—worried. She had sensed that my words to her were more integral now. No longer punctured with fear and need.

"There's other stuff I haven't told you, though."

"Like what?"

A noise in the distance made her jump. She looked around. Then she turned back to me.

"My father beat me."

"You told me that too."

"But I didn't tell you about my mother."

"No."

"When I was little, she was sick. Really sick. That's why I was raised by my grandmother."

I said, "I'm sorry," but I only felt sorry for myself. A limit had been passed. Every relationship has an expiration date for regurgitating traumas and confessions, past which empathy can no longer be asked for. Disinterested understanding at most.

"I didn't know she was sick, because she'd been sick since before I was born and so I thought all mothers ate medication the way cats eat kibble. I thought all moms periodically disappeared, disappeared into hospitals. And that you had to wait for them without eating otherwise they wouldn't come back."

"Without eating?"

"Yes. That's what I said."

"I thought all moms, if they were tired, used a wheel-chair. I thought they had smart friends with stethoscopes who came to check if they felt good, make sure their body was all right . . ."

I stared at her unguarded expression. Her tense shoulders. Her whole posture. I'd never seen her like that. I felt sorry for her. But it felt far away, like a suddenly remembered movie.

"It wasn't a terminal illness my mother had, but it wasn't treated right when she was little and so she never really recovered. Then when I was ten it got worse and I only ever saw her horizontal, on a bed or a cot. All my dolls were always horizontal. How were yours?"

"Ugly. I played more with my brother's blocks. But I don't want to talk about that now."

"What do you want to talk about then?" Her smile was sad and hopeful.

"Nothing, Xu. I don't want to talk to you about anything. I'm leaving."

"No. Please. You can't go like that. You're too fucked up."

"Don't pretend you give a shit about that. You just don't want me to leave."

"No. I don't need anyone."

"This sham again? Will you give it up? Is it really so hard for you to be sincere? Vulnerable, real?"

"You're too cold. Too cold. Harsh. This isn't what I want."

She dropped her face in her hands. Her fragility was repulsive. Then, something came through the door. A dark shadow, moving, low. Cats. Dozens of cats. They scattered throughout the hall, meowing. One came up to Xu and sniffed her hand.

"Come here," she implored.

I bent toward her. She was still kneeling like a cheap groom figurine on a wedding cake. I kissed her. A wet, bitter kiss. Her mouth tasted cold. Then something came over me. I bit her lip. She jerked back, shocked, and lifted her hand to the trickle of blood. She offered her hand to the cat to lick. I gathered my things and went to leave.

Xu watched me walk away, still crouching next to the cat. At the door, I turned around: all you could see were cats, a shapeless, teeming mass. She was in the shadows, invisible. I felt a pang of sorrow I miraculously managed to deflect.

When I got home, The Jing'an Temple of Peace and Tranquility was still lit. It was a holiday: on holidays everything is lit up. I didn't know which holiday. People packed the streets, prey to some frenzy. I thought I wouldn't be able to sleep that night, but I'd feel better in time. In time, everything gets better. It always does. Construction sites become candy stores, excess flab around the middle shrinks down, restoring the skeleton's contours. Children become adults, and adults, eventually, stop being children. Childhood closes up: a scar, rough, desensitized, it doesn't hurt anymore. Loves become memories of places and experiences, parts of bodies. Xu would become something like that. In my head. Something cold. An idea.

In bed, I couldn't fall asleep: outside there was too much light, too much life. Tomorrow, I would have to ask reception for some curtains, some blinds. A way to block everything out. I got up and drank some chemical tap water—I was out of bottles. Everything outside was still illuminated. I thought that Shanghai was like a brain drunk on lack of rest. I thought that it was wonderful and painful and it made me wish I were anywhere else. Anyone else. I set the picture of me and Ruben by the window, where the festive glow could reach us, flood us with light.

30

Hands

Love isn't a human thing. Fish love the sea with their gills, a love so tyrannical that a few seconds away from it is enough to kill them. Bats have such unpleasant faces because their bodies have loved darkness to the point of deformation. Jellyfish melt instantly in a sunlight they hadn't known they desired. Ants march single file out of desperate longing for a crumb. Cats leave our ankles with little bites like stamps, loving us with a love that's only visible when superimposed by pain.

I don't remember exactly what happened in the ten days that followed. I remember the floor was strewn with newspapers I hadn't thrown out. One of them announced a new coffee bar opening at the slaughterhouse. The photo showed a never-ending line, people waiting with rapt looks, but it was another place, another slaughter-house, another city. I remember rewatching the TV shows I already knew by heart. Knowing the lines was comforting. A mental lullaby. I ate old vegetables and mushy, unfeeling fruit. Little brown apples and pears that hurt my teeth. I talked to my parents every afternoon. We saw each other on screen, on Skype. They said, "You've gotten prettier." I gave them other, similarly kind compliments, and their house, my house, in the back-ground, looked different, the same but more abstract, like a house in a dream. I took walks, but only after sundown. I looked at the dark shop windows. Days alter-nated with nights, the way they always do, even when you're falling out of love.

It took me six days to decide to return to Rome, and three to buy the plane ticket. As I stared at the screen, the possible dates and times seemed as menacing and senseless as the signs over the safety exits that at night, in the hall, occasionally went off unprompted. But I had decided. A circle had closed, and it didn't matter whether it made sense to me. When a circle closes, you fall away from geometry a little, but then you're forced to find another shape. Emma and Olga provided moral support via email, promising me drinks and laughs and shopping and calm. A future of sorts. I thanked them and acted hopeful, confident, resolved.

The call came at three in the morning. It was Xu, crying, on the other end of the phone. No, it wasn't Xu. It was a girl with a voice similar to hers, but a bit sharper. She said, "Come to Xu's." I was sitting on the edge of the bed; I could feel my head spinning in disorientation. "What happened?" I said. "I'll tell you later. This is Biyu." I was stunned, speechless. "Kelly," she said, almost shouting, thinking I hadn't understood.

I dressed quickly, my heart in my throat, after trying uselessly to call back. I tripped over my suitcase, already by the door, with my backpack on top and a printout of my plane ticket. I hailed a taxi. I dialed up and raced to the elevator. The door was open. For a moment I wondered if I was still dreaming. Was it a harmless night-mare, reversible, like the others?

I went inside. I saw Kelly from behind, in the shadow, her back to me. A grotesque pile of yellow hair: a little girl dressed up as Sailor Moon. My words caught in my throat. She was looking on the floor. On the floor was Xu. Eyes closed, palm open, a little pile of yellow pills.

"D-Did you . . . Did you call an ambulance??"

Kelly slowly turned around. I had a strange feeling. Like she had different faces. One for each name. All the faces pieced together, all the names pieced together from so many fragments that all together made her expression indecipherable. There was a smile, a hint of sadness, something inconsolable, and maybe a touch of curiosity.

"Of course. But I called you first."

I knelt over her.

"Xu. Xu, say something, please."

"Ruben. You need to know, Xu loves you, the thing with me was nothing."

"I don't care. This isn't the time."

I took her head in my hands. I didn't know what to do.

"I know. But I wanted to tell you."

I was so nauseous I couldn't breathe. I shook her shoulders. Then I felt a tremor. An electric current that sparked in her neck and flared into my fingers. She was alive. With a convulsion, she turned to her side and threw up. I laughed with joy and relief. Kelly squealed and went to get some paper towels. She cleaned Xu's mouth. Soon after that we heard the ambulance siren.

"I'll go with her," I said. Kelly nodded, smiling. I thought she was pretty and I'd never noticed, and that garish, unnatural hair color looked good on her. I thought, in the span of a second, of all the possible forms of love, like all the wavelengths of light. In the ambulance I held Xu's hand the entire way, a span of time that seemed drawn out and bittersweet, like your first day of school. Xu's eyes drooped and she squeezed my hand tight. The ride was bumpy; the ambulance seemed to soar up in the air then plonk down, and for some reason it made me want to laugh. Xu's eyes widened like a saint having a holy vision and she said, "Wo ai ni," which means "I love you"—although the ideogram for *love* contains the one for *claws*, and *night*, an infinite darkness, if you analyze it, if you really want to analyze everything, which is the worst problem with being alive and human—and I said it back the same way, "Wo ai ni," careful with my pronunciation, careful to make sure that she believed my words, just as I had believed hers. The ambulance doors opened onto a giant parking lot, a hospital, a sky of twisting colors. "Now will you tell me what your name is?" Xu asked. She smiled, I smiled. The sun was on the horizon.

A NOTE ON THE AUTHOR
AND TRANSLATOR

Viola Di Grado's novels include the Strega finalist and Premio Campiello award–winning *70% Acrylic 30% Wool* and *Hollow Heart*, a finalist for the PEN Literary Award for Translation. She holds a degree in Eastern languages from the University of Turin and a master's in East Asian philosophy from the University of London. She lives in London.

Jamie Richards is a translator and editor based in Milan. She holds an MFA from the University of Iowa and a PhD from the University of Oregon. A 2021 NEA fellowship recipient, she has translated works by Roberto Saviano, Igiaba Scego, and others.